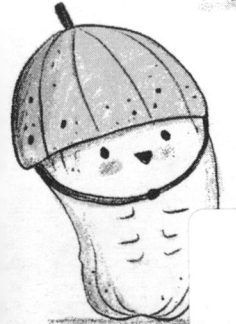

*For Janet. Thank you for always being so kind and dedicated to Amelia Fang. Pumpkin hugs always xxx*

# AMELIA FANG

## and the

## NAUGHTY CATICORNS

LAURA ELLEN ANDERSON

**EGMONT**

First published in Great Britain in 2020
by Egmont UK Limited
2 Minster Court, 10th floor, London EC3R 7BB

Text and illustrations copyright © 2020 Laura Ellen Anderson

The moral rights of the author and illustrator have been asserted

ISBN 978 1 4052 9703 5

70765/001

Printed and bound in Great Britain by CPI Group

MIX
Paper from
responsible sources
FSC® C020471

# CONTENTS

ETRIFIED FOREST
FLORENCE'S PIT
AUNT MAVIS'S PIT
ZOMBIE YOGA HALL
CENTRAL NOCTURNIA GRAVEYARD
THE PETRIFIED-TREE-THAT-LOOKS-LIKE-A-UNICORN
THE HAUNTED HOUSES
TOAD BRIDGE
THE FANG MANSION

# Ghoulish Greetings!

## AMELIA FANG

**AND SQUASHY**

**LIKES:**
Her special pumpkin ornament
Making shows with friends

**DISLIKES:**
The thought of being
a terrible sister

**LIKES:**
Opera singing
Wearing Countess
Frivoleeta's shoes

**DISLIKES:**
Pumpy being in danger
Losing precious shoes

## TANGINE

**AND PUMPY**

**LIKES:**
Unicornelius Pine toys
Prancing in a tutu

**DISLIKES:**
Naughty caticorns
Disrespecting Unicornelius Pine

## FLORENCE

## GRIMALDI

**LIKES:**
Putrid pancakes
Spreading toe jam with
his scythe

**DISLIKES:**
Too many creatures crying
Things making him jump

## WOOO

**LIKES:**
Helping Amelia and friends
His motorcycle helmet
collection

**DISLIKES:**
Being vacuumed up
Being frozen in a jar

## AUNT LAVITORA

**LIKES:**
Her messenger crow 'Monroe'
Her business 'Manors &
Morgues'

**DISLIKES:**
Cheap stockings
Being disturbed when counting

**LIKES:**
Dancing and climbing around
Playing music and drawing

**DISLIKES:**
Being ignored
Bring given new toys

## GERRARD    BUTLER    MO

# CHAPTER 1

# DROP BREAD GORGEOUS

It was a delightfully dreary Saturday evening. Amelia Fang munched on a bowl of Unlucky Arms cereal with her two best friends, Florence and Grimaldi. The big fluffy yeti and tiny grim reaper were staying over at the Fang Mansion for a weekend of frightful fun.

'O.M.GENIES!' cried Florence, picking up the box of Unlucky Arms. 'YOU CAN WIN A LIMITED EDITION UNICORNELIUS PINE TOY?!'

Grimaldi Reaperton gasped and almost choked on his putrid pancake. 'I LOVE Unicornelius Pine of Rainbow River!'

he spluttered. 'I've watched ALL the episodes on Deathflix, and Grimama says she'll get me a Unicornelius Pine jumper if I pass my Toad Trials this Halloween!'

Amelia read the back of the packet. *'To win your very own Unicornelius Pine toy, all YOU have to do is find a silver unicorn horn in your cereal box . . .'*

Florence grabbed the box and tipped the whole thing upside down. Green and blue arm-shaped cereal scattered across the tabletop and on to the floor. Amongst it all, just next to Grimaldi's plate, glimmered something small and shiny. Florence gasped and lurched forward, grabbing the tiny object.

'THAT'S NO 'ORN! IT'S A STAR,' said Florence, looking dejected. 'WHAT DO YOU GET WITH A STAR?'

Amelia studied the back of the cereal box and eventually found the answer in the small

print. *'If you find the precious star, then SMILE. It's YOURS, because Unicornelius Pine thinks you are ALL stars!'*

Grimaldi smiled. 'We're staaaars!' he said gleefully. 'That's the best prize ever!'

'I FINK I MIGHT VOMIT,' said Florence flatly. 'I DON'T WANNA BE TOLD I'M SHINY AN' AMAZING. I WANT THE TOY.' She hurrumphed and carried on munching handfuls of cereal straight from the table.

'So, what do you guys want to do first?' asked Amelia. 'Maybe we could take Squashy for a bounce to the Pumpkin Patch? I've heard there are lots of baby pumpkins sprouting up at the moment!' Amelia's pet pumpkin, Squashy, waggled his stalk enthusiastically at this idea.

'Speaking of babies,' said Grimaldi, 'how much longer until your new brother or sister arrives?'

'Hopefully th—' Amelia began, before being cut off by a very familiar voice.

'The toilet seat STILL ISN'T SHINY ENOUGH!' Countess Frivoleeta's shrill voice echoed through the Fang Mansion.

Amelia flinched. 'Hopefully the baby will be here soon,' she continued in a hushed voice. 'Now Mum's expecting a baby, she's acting so *weird*. She won't stop eating Foot Fudge and she never even liked it before! And then one minute she's all happy and laughing, and the next she's crying. And NOTHING is shiny enough any more. *NOTHING!*'

Grimaldi shot an anxious look at his slightly toe-jam-smeared and not-very-shiny scythe blade.

Amelia gave an excitable wriggle. 'But I REALLY hope the baby hurries up because I can't wait to be a big sister!'

'THAT'S WELL EXCITING!' bellowed Florence through a mouthful of breakfast. 'I WISH I 'AD A LITTLE BRUVVA OR SISTER. I'D TEACH 'EM 'OW TO BE THE BEST PRANCER IN THE KINGDOMS!' Even though Florence was huge, she pranced as if she were as light as a feather. It was a very impressive sight.

'If I had a little grim-brother or sister, I'd teach them how to sweep up dead toads without leaving a slimy mess,' said Grimaldi, spreading some more toe jam on to his putrid pancake.

'NICE,' said Florence with a grimace. 'AN' YOU JUST USED THE SAME SCYTHE FOR SPREADING JAM THAT YOU USE TO SWEEP UP SQUISHED TOADS!'

'I cleaned it on my cloak hood first,' said Grimaldi, gazing innocently at Florence.

Amelia chuckled. 'I can't wait to introduce my baby brother or sister to you guys!' she said. Squashy pa-doinged into Amelia's lap and blew a raspberry.

'And of course, the baby will be *very* excited to meet YOU!' Amelia said, tickling Squashy's tummy. He squeaked and smiled.

Amelia's mother waddled into the kitchen. She had a very large tummy indeed, her usually immaculate beehive hairdo was a tangled mess, and her eyeballs were in the wrong sockets. She walked straight over to the fridge.

'WHERE IS MY FOOT FUDGE?!' she squawked, searching through half-eaten tubs of splattered spleen and mushy brain balls.

'Uh oh,' Amelia whispered to her friends. 'I think Dad forgot to buy more fudge . . .'

Countess Frivoleeta turned around and gave Amelia a wobbly-eyed stern look. 'WHO ate the last of my –' Luckily, just at that moment, Amelia's dad came running into the kitchen holding a big, stripy cardboard box.

'HERE, my disastrous little wart-picker!' said Count Drake, trying to catch his breath. He opened the box to reveal a freshly made batch of Foot Fudge. 'I dashed to your favourite bakery, *Drop Bread Gorgeous*. And *look*, there are extra-crusty bits from in between the toes, just how you like it!'

Countess Frivoleeta's bottom lip trembled. Then she sat down at the kitchen table and burst into tears.

Count Drake put an arm around his wife. 'Why are you crying, darkling? I thought you'd be happy about the extra-crusty fudge?'

'NO! It's not *that* . . .' said the countess as a long strand of snot dangled from her right nostril. 'I just remembered something I saw last week. There was a mouldy bean on the ground outside. It was all by itself. So small . . . and mouldy . . . and bean-like!'

She let out a loud wail. Amelia, Florence and Grimaldi all tried very hard not to laugh.

## BOOOOOOOONG!

The door gong echoed loudly through the Fang Mansion, covering the sound of the gang's muffled laughter.

'Are we expecting guests?' asked Count Drake, sounding quite relieved at the interruption.

'Maybe Wooo is back early from visiting

his brother?' said Amelia.

Wooo was the Fang family's ghost butler. He kept everything in the Fang Mansion in order. But once a year he would take a well-deserved minibreak to visit his travelling brother, Fantom. Without Wooo around, things could get a little chaotic and messy, especially now that Amelia's parents were distracted with preparations for the new baby.

Countess Frivoleeta suddenly stopped crying. Her eyes grew so wide that Amelia feared they might fall out.

*'Bothering bogeymen!'* the countess shrieked. 'That'll be my sister, Lavitora. I completely forgot that I'd agreed to babysit her caticorns while she goes on an important work trip.' She began shovelling handfuls of Foot Fudge into her mouth. 'How on earth are we meant to look after three tiny creatures when we still have so much to get ready for

*our* new baby?! He or she could be born any night now!' Both Countess Frivoleeta's eyeballs finally popped out on to the floor, rolling over to where Amelia stood.

'It's all right, Mum,' Amelia said, wiping down her mum's eyeballs and handing them back. 'Florence, Grimaldi and I can help look after the caticorns while you and Dad take care of the baby stuff.'

The thought of looking after three fluffy little caticorns sounded like SO much fun. Amelia could already imagine them following her everywhere as her mum and dad looked on, telling each other what a brilliant big sister she would make!

'What do you think, guys?' Amelia smiled a big, fang-filled grin at her friends.

'EASY-PEASY!' declared Florence breezily.

'And I'm very good with little creatures,' said Grimaldi.

'WELL, DEAD ONES ANYWAY,' Florence pointed out.

'Oh, thank you, my horrible little bin-lids,' said Count Drake, smiling at everyone gratefully and putting an arm around Amelia. 'That would be a massive help!' He turned to the countess. 'See, dear, everything's going to work out *juuuust* fine.'

'Oh, Amelia,' said Countess Frivoleeta, stroking her daughter's cheek and smearing Foot Fudge across it. 'All grown-up . . . and . . . and . . .'

'I FINK SHE'S GUNNA CRY AGAIN,' Florence whispered loudly.

But before Frivoleeta had a chance to bawl her eyes out, a loud DONK DONK DONK filled the room, making her jump.

Grimaldi yelped and hid under the table as a face appeared at the kitchen window behind him.

'COOO-EEEEEE!' said a large prim-and-proper-looking lady. *'Is anyone going to let us in?'*

'I really need to get used to answering the front door while Wooo is away,' sighed Count Drake. He waved at the window. 'Be right there, Lavitora!' he called, before muttering under his breath, 'Do we *have* to let her in?'

'I'll get it!' said Amelia, very excited at the thought of meeting her aunt's little caticorns. Florence and Grimaldi followed, eager to meet the new guests, with Squashy pa-doinging along close behind.

Amelia pulled open the heavy wooden front door. 'Hi, Aunt Lavitora!'

'DAAAAAAAAAAAAAAAAAAARKLING!' Aunt Lavitora's shrill voice resonated through the house like nails scraping along a chalkboard.

Wearing a high-collared gothic dress with frills in places you'd never imagine,

Aunt Lavitora strutted into the entrance hall carrying a large suitcase in one gloved hand and a bunch of withered roses in the other. She looked like a version of Countess Frivoleeta who had been stretched widthways. A messenger crow with a top hat and a monocle perched on her shoulder.

'Amelia Fang!' Aunt Lavitora oozed. 'You were just a disgusting wrinkly little thing last time I saw you!' Then she called over her shoulder, 'Come on in, my little floofs!'

Amelia's eyes widened as three caticorns with fluffy fur and shiny little horns trailed through the door. Amelia squealed in excitement. As they stood in a neat row, smiling sweetly, she thought that they were the

most adorable creatures she'd ever set eyes upon (aside from Squashy of course!). Looking after them was going to be *such* a treat.

'Amelia, darkling,' said Aunt Lavitora. 'Meet Gerrard, Butler and Mo.'

# CHAPTER 2

# GERRARD, BUTLER AND MO

Gerrard, who was wearing a small, frilly collar, twirled on the spot. Butler tapped a little tune with his claws and pinged the bow around his neck, and Mo – who was wearing a cute knitted jumper – adjusted her glasses before drawing an imaginary heart in the air with her paws.

Amelia thought her cold vampiric heart might just explode with love.

'Hi, Gerrard. Hi, Butler. Hi, Mo!' she said to each caticorn in turn. 'I'm Amelia! And this is my pet pumpkin Squashy, and my best friends, Florence and Grimaldi.'

'ALWITE, VERY SMALL CATS!' said Florence with a wave. 'OR DO YOU PREFER TO BE CALLED UNICORNS? OR UNICATS?' She scratched her head. 'THIS IS COMPLICATED.'

'They're *caticorns*, dear!' declared Aunt Lavitora. Then she leaned in and dabbed Florence's nose with one finger. 'And what a delightful beast you are!' she cooed.

Amelia put her head in her hands. *Uh oh*, she thought.

Florence straightened up and puffed out her chest.

'I AM NOT A BEAST!' she said loudly.

The caticorns whimpered. Florence spotted this and said as quietly as she could muster (which was still very loud indeed), 'I'M A *RARE BREED* OF YETI!'

Then she bent down and patted the caticorns

in turn. 'SORRY, TINY UNICORN KITTIES, IT'S SUMFIN' I SIMPLY 'AVE TO DO WHENEVER ANYONE SAYS THAT B-WORD.'

Aunt Lavitora stood in shocked silence. Amelia tried not to laugh.

'Hellooooo, Gerrard, Butler and Mo! It's very nice to meet you!' said Grimaldi, trying to ease the tension. He waved his scythe around, narrowly missing Gerrard's horn. The caticorns yelped and hid behind Lavitora's skirt. 'Oops, sorry about that!' said Grimaldi, looking embarrassed. He put the scythe behind his back.

'Now, now,' said Lavitora, ushering the caticorns out from behind her. 'Don't be silly. Let's show Amelia, the *rare breed* and Gary-Mouldy just how brave and brilliant you are.'

Florence narrowed her eyes. Grimaldi blushed.

Lavitora straightened Mo's glasses, before addressing Amelia. 'I literally JUST picked up my little darklings from *Batwings Boarding School for the Bright and Beaming*!' she said. 'Best school in the Kingdoms of the Dark *and* the Light, you know! They're taught how to be polite and proper little creatures there, so I'm sure they'll be *very* well behaved for you.'

Aunt Lavorita leaned forward so that the smell of her rotten raspberry perfume filled Amelia's nostrils. 'Here's a suitcase full of gifts to keep them happy. There should be enough to amuse my precious little floofs for the whole night! I shall be back by moonset.'

She shoved the large suitcase into Amelia's arms, then turned to her crow and said, 'Monroe, did Professor McShady reply to my message about the cloud complex?'

Gerrard tugged on Aunt Lavitora's skirt. 'Mew,' he said.

'In a moment, darkling,' said Aunt Lavitora, waving a hand at the little caticorn.

'SQUAAAAAAAAAWK!' replied the crow.

'Thank you, Monroe,' said Lavitora. Then she looked at Amelia and smiled. 'Sorry about that. Being the boss of *Manors and Morgues* just takes up ALL of my time. Especially when the wealthiest leprechaun in the Kingdom of the Light wants to talk about building a new cloud complex in Glitteropolis! I am just sooooooo busy!'

Amelia couldn't think of anything more boring than building a cloud complex. 'I'd really like to be a pumpkinologist when I grow up,' she said proudly.

Aunt Lavitora burst out laughing. 'You strange little thing! You don't want to do a grubby job like that!'

Amelia frowned and was about to respond crossly when her mother shuffled into the entrance hall.

'Sister!' called Countess Frivoleeta. She greeted Aunt Lavitora with a floaty kiss on both cheeks. *'So awful to see you!'*

'It's been TOO LONG, Frivvy!' said Aunt Lavitora.

'Only ten years,' mumbled Count Drake.

Countess Frivoleeta stamped on his toe.

Lavitora held out the bunch of withering roses to her sister. *'Here!'* she said.

Countess Frivoleeta looked surprised. 'Oh! You shouldn't have!' she said as a dead petal fell gently to the floor.

Aunt Lavitora chuckled. 'Oh, I didn't!' she said. 'These are for ME. I just need you to hold them whilst I pull up my *very* expensive stockings. The roses were a treat to

myself for selling *another* house in the Rickety Residences. Y'know, I've sold THIRTEEN AND A HALF houses in that area *alone*. AND I was just telling Amelia here about a very exciting deal with Professor McShady – the *wealthiest* leprechaun in the Kingdom of the Light!' She yanked at her shimmering stocking and then took the flowers back.

Count Drake pretended to yawn and fall asleep. He sneaked a wink at Amelia, who tried very hard not to giggle.

'Oh. That *is* very exciting to hear, sister,' said Countess Frivoleeta flatly. 'We're all fine, by the way, in case you were wondering . . .' But then she spotted the caticorns and gasped. 'Goodness me, is that Gerrard, Butler and Mo?' The countess leaned in a little closer and smiled sweetly. 'It's so lovely to finally meet you!'

'They're divine, aren't they?' said Aunt

Lavitora absent-mindedly, pulling out a notebook from her top pocket and scribbling down some big numbers.

Butler tapped Aunt Lavitora on the elbow, trying to get her attention.

'Not now, snookipoop,' said Lavitora. 'Mummy has important business to attend to.'

Countess Frivoleeta cleared her throat. 'Well, would you like to stay for a cup of scream tea before you go?'

Not taking her eyes off her notebook, Aunt Lavitora held up a hand and carried on counting. Mo meowed and pulled on her frills.

'Not yet, floofy!' snapped Aunt Lavitora.

Monroe the crow squawked twice. 'SQUAAAAWK! SQUAAAAWK!'

'Oh, really?' replied Lavitora. Then she looked at her sister and smiled. 'I'd *love* to stay, but I must dash!' Count Drake let out a sigh of relief. 'Gerrard, Butler, Mo . . . be good

little caticorns, won't you?' said Aunt Lavitora.

The caticorns nodded in unison.

'Well, Amelia is going to help look after Gerrard, Butler and Mo,' said Countess Frivoleeta proudly. 'And she'll show them what a FANGTASTIC big sister she's going to be for this little one!' She patted her tummy pointedly.

'Oh, of course!' gushed Aunt Lavitora. 'How could I forget that you have a new little vampire on the way? I did wonder why you were looking more tired than usual.'

Countess Frivoleeta's left eyeball twitched, but she smiled stiffly. 'Well, you probably won't have time to stay for a scream tea when you come to collect the caticorns at moonset, will you?'

Aunt Lavitora laughed. 'Ha! Probably not, darkling sister of mine. I'm a very busy woman after all!' She then whispered, not very quietly, 'Plus, I do find your Drakey terribly drab . . .'

The count spluttered indignantly.

Aunt Lavitora opened the door. 'Monroe!' she said to her crow. 'Please fly ahead and tell Professor McShady I'm on my way.'

*'I'll see you later then!'* called Countess Frivoleeta, but Lavitora was already at the end of the path. The countess sighed. Amelia thought she looked a little bit relieved but decided not to say anything. Count Drake, on the other hand, made his feelings quite clear as he fist-pumped the air.

'Right, your father and I have a list as long

as a bogeyman's snot trail to get through before the new baby arrives!' said the countess. She placed a hand on Amelia's shoulder and smiled. 'Are you *sure* you don't mind taking care of the caticorns, my little pimple-popper?'

'Not a problem!' said Amelia.

'AN' WE'RE 'ERE TO 'ELP TOO!' said Florence with a salute.

'Yup!' said Grimaldi, spinning his scythe and almost knocking a picture off the wall.

'You're all disastrously delightful. Thank you!' said Countess Frivoleeta, tears welling up in her eyes. Then she turned to Count Drake and cleared her throat. 'Before I start crying again, you grab the orange paint for the baby's room, and the Foot Fudge.'

'Why do we need the Foot Fudge?' asked Count Drake.

'For me to eat whilst I watch you paint,

of course!'

Amelia's mum and dad headed out of the hall, leaving Amelia, Florence and Grimaldi with the caticorns. Squashy waggled his stalk and squeaked at the three little guests to say hello, but the caticorns didn't react.

'THEY'RE WEIRDLY QUIET,' said Florence. Then she leaned towards Amelia and lowered her voice, unsuccessfully. 'ALSO, 'OW COME YOU'VE NEVER MET 'EM TIL NOW?' she asked.

'Well, we've not actually seen Aunt Lavitora since I was a baby,' said Amelia. 'She is very busy and important apparently.'

'SOUNDS WELL BORIN',' said Florence.

'I agree,' said Amelia. 'But boring is NOT on *our* agenda! We're going to have *fun*!' She knelt down so that she was level with the little caticorns. 'Want to go play zombie tag in the back graveyard?'

The caticorns looked at each other and nodded enthusiastically.

But they were suddenly interrupted by an almighty cry from upstairs.

'THE BABY IS COMING!'

# CHAPTER 3

# WE ARRANGED A DOOR

'RUMBLING RACOONS! I need to get to the Nocturnia Infirmary *right now*!' Amelia's mother shrieked. 'Drakey-poos? WHERE ARE YOU, MY AWFUL LITTLE HAIR FOLLICLE?'

'Be right there, my disgusting daymare!' called the count, running up the stairs, still embracing a box of Foot Fudge.

Amelia, Florence, Grimaldi and the caticorns raced up the stairs behind him.

'SHOULD WE CALL A DOCTOR?' asked Florence.

'No need!' said the count. 'We arranged a door on the third floor. It'll lead us straight to the infirmary.'

'Neat!' said Grimaldi.

The doors in the Fang Mansion had a tendency to move around a lot and lead to different places. Amelia was lucky if her bedroom door stayed in the same place for more than a few weeks!

On the third floor of the Fang Mansion there was now a shiny white door with a green cross on it. The countess was leaning with one hand on the door handle looking a little bit hot and sweaty, but at least she had a big smile on her face.

'It's *time*, darklings!' she huffed and puffed. '*The baby is on its way!*'

Amelia felt her insides do a somersault.

'This is SO exciting!' she said happily, giving her mum a big hug but being careful not to squish her tummy too much.

'I'm going to call Wooo to ask him to come back so he can look after you all while we're away at the infirmary,' said Count Drake. 'Hopefully it won't take him long to return, but will you be okay for a little while on your own with the caticorns?'

'No worries, Dad,' said Amelia. She gestured towards the caticorns. 'I don't think we'll have any problems here. I mean, *look at them*. They're being as good as goblin slime!'

Gerrard, Butler and Mo, who were holding paws, smiled and meowed sweetly.

'Well, hopefully we'll be back sooner rather than later,' Count Drake said, giving Amelia one last cuddle and opening the white door with the green cross. 'Be good until Wooo gets here!'

Amelia waved as her parents walked through the door and into the shiny black hallways of the Nocturnia Infirmary. Her head was swirling with excitable thoughts. She was going to be a BIG SISTER! Would she have a little brother or sister? What would they look like? What would Mum and Dad name the new baby vampire?!

Amelia shook her head and composed herself. She had three little caticorns to take care of. And *this* was her chance to show everyone what a FANGTASTIC big sister she was going to be!

'I know!' said Amelia. 'Why don't we all go watch a glittery movie until Wooo arrives?'

Gerrard looked at Butler, who looked at Mo. And then all three caticorns nodded once.

'Well, that was easy!' said Amelia. 'You really are very good little caticorns!' She smiled and ruffled their furry heads affectionately.

'OOO, 'AVE YOU GOT *THE DAYMARE BEFORE HALLOWEEN*?!' asked Florence. 'THAT'S ONE OF ME FAVOURITE MOVIES.'

'Let's go have a look,' said Amelia. 'If we head to the unliving room, we can all choose a movie together!'

As Amelia, Squashy, Florence, Grimaldi and the caticorns strode down the hall, one of the doors began to rumble and swirl. Then it turned into a pizza. Gerrard, Butler and Mo gasped.

'Oh, the doors in our house are a little odd,' Amelia explained to the confused-looking caticorns. 'They move around and sometimes do strange things like bursting into bubbles or turning into popcorn!' She carried on along the corridor, pointing to various doors. 'We call this door Jane because it looks a bit like one of Mum's friends called Jane – funny, right?!' She laughed. But there was silence. 'Well, I thought it was fun –'

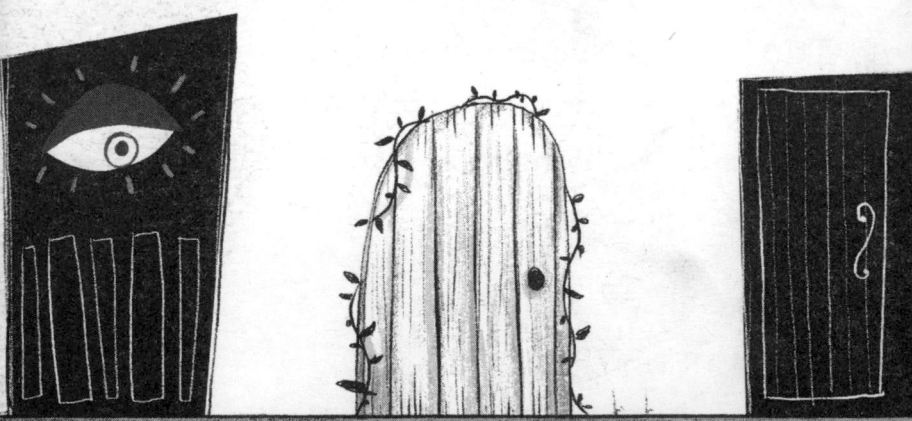

'UM, AMELIA . . .' interrupted Florence. 'WHERE DID THE CATICORNS GO?'

'That's odd,' said Grimaldi. 'They were right behind us a second ago.'

'Gerrard? Butler? Mo?' Amelia called out. Then she noticed that the pizza door was gone. Squashy squeaked and pointed his stalk towards a trail of crumbs.

'DID THEY . . . *EAT* THE PIZZA DOOR?' asked Florence, scratching her head.

'Um, I think so!' said Amelia in disbelief.

Amelia and her friends followed the trail of pizza crumbs along the corridor until they reached a large door with a big eyeball for a door handle.

'I was really hoping they hadn't gone through *this* door,' said Amelia, grimacing. She reached towards the eyeball door handle, hoping it wouldn't burst in her hand like it usually did.

But then another door opened. The three caticorns zoomed out of it, riding

SHHH

on a vacuum cleaner. Gerrard was steering, wearing Countess Frivoleeta's favourite silk gown as a cape. Butler was using a toilet-roll tube as a trumpet and Mo was brandishing two tubes of glitter paint. They whizzed along the corridor, approaching Amelia and her friends at speed.

Amelia, Florence and Grimaldi managed to jump out of the way just in time, as the caticorns zipped past on the vacuum. Mo made sure to spray the friends with as much glitter as possible as she passed.

'AAAAAARGH, WHAT JUST HAPPENED?!' said Florence, wiping herself down. 'I FORT YOUR AUNT SAID THEY WERE WELL BEHAVED?!'

'I don't know. Maybe they're just over-excited?' said Amelia, wracking her

brain for answers. 'But one thing's for sure. We can't let the caticorns out of our sight!'

Amelia, Florence and Grimaldi ran along the corridor, following the trail of freshly vacuumed carpet and glitter splats. It finally led them through a big, furry yellow door and out into the back graveyard.

'Grieving gobblepots!' said Amelia. 'We've been babysitting for barely five minutes, and we've already lost the caticorns!'

# CHAPTER 4

# SAVED BY THE BONG

'Look!' said Grimaldi, pointing upwards.

'Pottering pumpkins!' Amelia cried.

Gerrard was swinging on the poison ivy that grew on the roof. Butler was sitting on the ledge of an open window playing Wooo's harmonica, and Mo was leaning precariously out of another window, writing (in the most intricate and beautiful lettering) the word 'BUM' on the side of the house with glitter paint.

'*GERRARD, BUTLER, MO!* Get down from there!' Amelia called up desperately. 'It's dangerous! You could

fall!' She couldn't believe this was happening, just as she was trying to prove what a brilliant big sister she could be.

Gerrard swung across the house on the vines before launching into one heart-dropping final somersault in mid-air.

Grimaldi fainted, collapsing to the floor amongst the gravestones and a panicked Amelia clung on to Florence's hairy arm.

But Gerrard flipped neatly into the window where Butler was playing the harmonica. Mo finished up her artwork, signing it with a neat 'M' and popped back into the house to join

her brothers.

Amelia and Florence breathed a massive sigh of relief and ran inside as fast as they could, dragging a recovering Grimaldi with them.

After racing up and down the spiral staircase, and in and out of various doors, Amelia finally caught the caticorns causing chaos in the kitchen.

Gerrard danced on the freezer, which seemed to be groaning, before slamming it shut and skipping on to a pile of dirty pots and pans. Butler rubbed his paws around the rims of different-sized drinking glasses to make eerie sounds and Mo was creating a very extravagant food sculpture.

Florence managed to gather the excitable caticorns under her arm and take them to the unliving room.

'Thanks Florence,'

Amelia breathed. She was sweating, which vampires hardly ever did. 'We have to find a way to calm them all down!'

'MAYBE WE SHOULD GIVE 'EM SOME PRESENTS FROM THE SUITCASE YOUR AUNT LEFT?' Florence suggested as Butler (still tucked under Florence's arm) attempted to use her belly as a drum. 'STOP THAT, LITTLE FLUFF MONSTER!' she said sternly.

'Good idea, Florence,' said Amelia, opening the suitcase. 'Look, Gerrard, Butler and Mo! Aunt Lavitora left some surprises for you!'

She passed an oddly shaped package to Gerrard. He ripped it open with his tiny caticorn claws and held up the gift.

Amelia made a weird choking noise.

Florence blurted out a rude word.

'Wow!' gasped Grimaldi. 'It can't be . . .'

Gerrard held up a VERY glittery unicorn toy, wearing a cape and wings. It was roughly the size of Grimaldi's head and had a squiggly signature on its cape.

'Is that . . .' whispered Grimaldi, who was desperately trying to keep a tube of glitter paint out of Mo's reach, 'is that a SIGNED *Unicornelius Pine of Rainbow River* toy?!'

'OH MY GOBLINS, THAT IS WELL COOL!' said Florence. 'HOW THE BATS DID YOUR AUNT GET THAT?'

'I can't even *imagine*!' breathed Amelia. 'It must have cost a squillion pounds!'

'You are so lucky!' Grimaldi breathed, floating around in wonder behind Gerrard.

Gerrard glanced at the toy then passed it to Butler, who threw it over to Mo. She shrugged and tossed it to the floor, chipping the unicorn's wing.

Amelia, Florence and Grimaldi took a sharp breath.

'That's NOT a very nice thing to do!' Amelia tried to sound strict. She wondered if this was how a big sister might deal with the situation. She put her hands on her hips in what she thought was probably a firm, big-sisterly manner.

Uni Corneluis.

'YEAH,' said Florence. 'THAT'S NO WAY TO TREAT UNICORNELIUS PINE!'

Gerrard looked at Amelia and then at Florence. His face crumpled and he began to cry. Butler and Mo took one look at Gerrard and began to cry too.

'ER, OKAY AMELIA,' said Florence taking a step backwards. 'THEY'RE ALL LEAKING WATER AN' I'M NOT SURE WHAT TO DO . . .'

Grimaldi pulled his hood over his eyes.

'I get anxious when more than two creatures cry at once!'

Amelia gulped. She wasn't sure what to do. She picked up Unicornelius Pine and waved him around in the air as if he were flying. 'Hey! *I'm Unicornelius Pine, and I'm here to save YOU!*' she said in a funny deep voice.

But the mewling cries grew louder. 'Please!' urged Amelia. 'There's no need to cry!'

'How do we make them stop?' Grimaldi had almost turned himself inside out in his effort to hide from the escalating noise.

BONG!

The caticorns stopped crying.

'Yessssss!' cheered Grimaldi. 'Saved by the bong!'

Then the caticorns began to cry again, except this time it was much louder with added kicking and screaming.

'That must be Wooo at the door,' said Amelia, feeling hopeful. 'He'll be able to help calm them down!'

But when Amelia opened the door, it wasn't the ghost butler waiting on the other side.

Prince Tangine La Floofle the First waltzed into the entrance hall with his arms outstretched. His genetically modified pet pumpkin, Pumpy, PA-DOOFED on to the doormat behind him, causing a great big *POOF*

of dust. Pumpy puffed out his chest, revealing an impressive six-pack.

Amelia sighed.

'Well, don't be TOO PLEASED to see me,' said Tangine, looking dejected.

'I'm sorry,' said Amelia, giving her friend a hug. 'I AM pleased to see you. I was just hoping it was Wooo – we're waiting for him to come back and we could REALLY do with his help right now.' Then she paused. 'I thought you had prince-training this weekend?'

Tangine – half-vampire, half-fairy – was the future king of Nocturnia and made sure everybody knew it. But even though he loved his own face far too much sometimes, he was one of Amelia's very best friends and always made her smile.

'Dad ate a bad batch of brain and is feeling sick,' said Tangine. 'So, I'm free to play with you guys instead. John the vulture dropped me off!'

The scraggly three-eyed vulture had collapsed in the front yard amongst the weeds. His eyes were looking in three different directions.

'He'll be fine,' said Tangine. 'So, what's going on?'

Amelia bit her lip.

'Well . . . my mum has gone to the infirmary to have the baby and we're looking after my aunt Lavitora's caticorns, who are a little trickier to handle than we first thought.'

Prince Tangine raised an eyebrow. 'Well, I'm sure these caticorns of yours will behave when they meet their FUTURE KING,' he said confidently . . .

## CHAPTER 5

# JAR OF WOOO

'What the bats?!' Tangine bellowed when he entered the unliving room.

The caticorns were rolling around on the floor in a frenzy. They were making an awful racket and flailing their paws around so that nobody could pick them up.

Pumpy bounced into the room with a PA-DOOF, but when he heard the screaming caticorns he swiftly PA-DOOFED right back out again.

Gerrard spun across the room and

accidentally bumped into a large wooden cabinet full of Count Drake's Crossword Critters trophies, causing the whole thing to wobble precariously. Florence just managed to stop the cabinet from tumbling over and squishing the little caticorn.

'THEY WON'T STOP MAKING THE NOISES!' said Florence with wide eyes. 'THEY'VE NOT TAKEN ONE BREF!'

Grimaldi was hiding under a cushion. 'What do we dooooo?!' he squeaked.

Squashy squidged himself as far under the sofa as he could.

'I told Gerrard off,' Amelia explained to a bewildered-looking Tangine. 'But not very much! Then he started crying, and then all THREE of them starting crying, and now they're having a full-on tantrum.'

'Why did you tell them off?' asked Tangine, dodging the hysterical caticorn's kicks.

'They threw their brand-new SIGNED Unicornelius Pine on to the floor, and *look* –' said Amelia, picking up the dented toy and passing it to Tangine – 'they chipped his wing!'

Tangine gasped. 'WELL! Then you deserve to be told off!' he called over to the caticorns, who clearly weren't listening. He shook his head disapprovingly. 'One should NEVER disrespect Unicornelius Pine!'

'EXACTLY,' Florence agreed.

Amelia paced back and forth. 'I think we . . . I . . . was maybe a bit too harsh?' Her mind was in a twizzle. 'But then, surely I have to tell them what's wrong and what's right?! I *am* responsible for them, after all.'

Amelia slumped on to the sofa, feeling very confused. Was having a baby brother or sister going to be *this* hard? She hadn't meant to upset the caticorns. She really hoped Wooo would hurry up and arrive soon to help her out.

'Amelia?' said Tangine. 'Are you okay?'

She stood up quickly. 'Yes!' she said, not entirely sure if this was the truth. 'Maybe the caticorns are hungry,' Amelia wondered out loud. 'Everyone gets a bit cranky when they're hungry, right?!'

'Oh yes, my Mummy Maids HAVE to meet my demands when I need food,' Tangine declared.

'*ONLY* WHEN YOU NEED FOOD?' Florence said with a smirk.

Tangine put a hand to his chest and gasped. 'I don't know WHAT you're suggesting, Florence, but it offends my delicate soul.'

Amelia ran to the kitchen as fast as she could and rummaged around in the deep, dark cupboards. Since Wooo had been away, and her parents had been so busy with baby preparations, keeping the place clean and tidy hadn't been top priority. There was now a rather unwieldy amount of creepy crawlies amongst the various food packages and even the odd cupboard troll lurking in the shadows.

Amelia eventually tracked down a few packets of assorted chilli scabs, cheese and bunion crisps and fried warts.

'That should do it!' she said to herself.

But then the sound of a faint moan stopped her in her tracks.

'Heeeeeeeeeeeelp . . .'

At first, Amelia thought it might be another pesky cupboard troll, but the voice sounded like it was coming from the freezer. The Fang Mansion had some weird quirks, but a talking freezer wasn't one of them.

Amelia waited in silence.

'Heeeeeeeeeeeelp . . .' came the voice again.

Unsure what else to do, Amelia replied, 'Hello? Who's there?'

'OoooooOOOOoooooooooooo.'

'Who?'

'OoooooooooOOOOOOOOOOOO
OOoooooooooooooooooooo!'

Amelia edged towards the
freezer slowly and leaned
in. Feeling a bit silly,
she said, 'I don't quite
understand. Can you please
repeat –'

'WOOOOOOOOOOOOOOO
OOOOOOOOO!'

'Wooooooooooooooo?' Amelia
muttered, scratching her head.
Then she gasped.

## 'WOOO!'

Amelia pulled open the freezer
door as fast as she could and there,
inside a glass jam jar, were two eyes
and a mouth complete with a cracked
monocle and a squished top hat.

It was Wooo. And he was frozen solid!

'Pottering pumpkins! Wooo, you poor thing!' Amelia shrieked, pulling the jar out of the freezer.

She unscrewed the lid and held the jar upside down above the kitchen table, but the solid block of ice-cold Wooo was very, very stuck.

'Y-y-young Amelia-a-a,' stuttered Wooo. His voice was muffled because of the glass and the fact he was frozen solid.

'What happened? I thought you were still travelling back,' said Amelia, placing the jar of Wooo on the kitchen table.

Wooo blinked a few times, then stuttered. 'I used a sh-sh-short cut to get here as f-f-f-fast as I could after your dad called me so that you w-w-wouldn't be left alone for t-t-t-too long.' Wooo's words created a small cloud of mist. 'I c-c-c-came in via a door on the t-t-t-top floor, and that's when I saw three c-c-caticorns riding around on the v-v-vacuum cleaner.'

Amelia felt her tummy twist. 'Oh no,' she said.

'I was v-v-vacuumed up before I had a chance to d-d-do anything, and then I w-w-woke up inside this j-j-j-j-j-j-jar in the freezer unable to m-m-move.'

When temperatures fell, a ghost lost their ability to pass through solid objects and would eventually turn into a block of paranormal ice. Which is exactly what had happened to Wooo.

Wooo looked like he was trying to smile. 'I m-m-must look very s-s-strange.'

'Oh, Wooo, how do we make you normal again?' asked Amelia.

'I j-j-just need to d-d-defrost, so b-b-best to leave me here in the warm and d-d-dry for a while,' said Wooo. 'I'm s-s-sorry I can't help you l-l-look after the c-c-caticorns.'

'*I'm* sorry you've been frozen!' said Amelia. 'I can't believe the caticorns did this to you! Aunt Lavitora told me they wouldn't be a problem. But they've been quite the opposite.' Amelia suddenly felt worried. 'Unless . . . unless they're only being naughty because of me. Maybe they don't like me?'

Just then Squashy and Pumpy appeared in the kitchen doorway. They were covered from stalk to bottom in multi-coloured paint. Squashy now had fat black eyelashes and a painted-on glittery beard. Pumpy looked very silly indeed, with a big red tomato stuck to the middle of his face and a LOT of lipstick around his mouth.

Squashy did NOT seem impressed by his new look. Pumpy, on the other hand, seemed to be embracing it, pouting at every opportunity. Squashy pa-doinged up and down and squeaked at Amelia frantically.

'What the bats has happened to you two?!' gasped Amelia. Although she knew *exactly* who was responsible for this. She turned to Wooo. 'I'd better go and see what's going on,' she said.

'G-g-g-go!' urged Wooo, who had begun to melt a little inside the jar.

Amelia's feet pounded along the corridor as she followed the freshly painted pumpkins back to the unliving room. What she saw next stopped her in her tracks.

Florence, Grimaldi and Tangine were bound together by a pink and black stripy rope, unable to move, and their faces were also covered in paint.

# CHAPTER 6
# STOP!

'WE GAVE 'EM ANOTHER PRESENT,' said Florence, who had stars painted all over her face. 'IT WAS A SKIPPING ROPE,' she continued. 'BUT THEY DIDN'T USE IT FOR SKIPPING . . . AS YOU CAN SEE.'

'They used it *against* us,' said Grimaldi, who had the word BUM painted across his forehead. He wriggled around, trying to break free from the rope.

'The one with the spiky collar – Gerald, is it? Well, he danced around us with the rope until we were dizzy just watching him,' said Tangine, wide-eyed. His eyes were painted to look like two huge flowers, with bright pink petals, he had a glittery splodge on his nose and two leaves on his cheeks. 'Then the other one with the little cape played a tune on a strange flute that made us all feel sleepy!'

'Next thing we knew, the skipping rope was wrapped around us,' Grimaldi continued.

'AND THEN MO PAINTED THE PUMPKINS!' Florence added.

'Um, the pumpkins aren't the *only* ones they painted,' Amelia said hesitantly.

Tangine yelped. 'Please tell me they haven't ruined my beautiful face?!'

Amelia bit her lip. 'It's not *completely* ruined . . .'

Tangine let out a strange noise in despair.

'But that's not important right now. Let me untie you guys. We need to go and find the caticorns. Which way did they go?' asked Amelia, fiddling with the tricky knots of the skipping rope.

'THEY RAN OFF!' said Florence. 'AN'

THEY DIDN'T EVEN BOVVA TO TAKE UNCORNELIUS PINE WIV 'EM!' She shook her head in disapproval. 'I'LL JUST 'AVE TO KEEP 'IM.'

'Hey, I thought we agreed that *I'd* have him,' said Grimaldi. 'You know how much I love Unicornelius Pine!'

'FINE! YOU CAN 'AVE 'IM AT WEEKENDS,' said Florence.

'Who CARES about Unicornelius Pine? You should be more concerned about my ruined face. MY PRECIOUS FACE!' wailed Tangine.

Amelia put her head in her hands. 'AARGH!' she cried. 'This is no good!'

Florence, Grimaldi and Tangine fell silent.

Amelia sighed. 'I'm sorry,' she said. 'It's just . . . the rope is knotted too tight, Wooo is frozen inside a jar and the caticorns are on a rampage. I don't know what to do!'

'Sorry, Amelia,' said Grimaldi. 'I would hug you, but it's a tad tricky right now.'

'RIGHT,' Florence said, with a look of determination. 'I KNEW THIS MOMENT WOULD COME EVENTUALLY.' She took a deep breath. 'AMELIA, STEP BACK. GRIMALDI, TANGINE, BRACE YERSELVES.'

'I would, but I'm TIED UP,' said Tangine sarcastically.

'What are you going to do?' asked Grimaldi, looking nervous.

'WHAT I SHOULD 'AVE DONE AGES AGO,' said Florence. With one massive grunt, she tensed every muscle in her body so that they

bulged and expanded. The skipping rope eventually snapped under the pressure, setting the friends free.

'THAT'S 'OW IT'S DONE!' said Florence proudly. 'NOW LET'S FIND THOSE KITTIES.'

'GERRAAAAAARD!' called Amelia.

'BUTLEEEEER!' yelled Grimaldi.

'Jo!' bellowed Tangine. 'Or is it Flo? Wait, what's the third one called?'

'MO!' said Florence, running for the door.

'Gerrard, Butler, Mo! Where are you?! *Please come back here, all of you!*' Amelia called out to nowhere in particular, in the hope that the caticorns could hear her. 'Otherwise, I'll have to tell Aunt Lavitora how naughty you've all been! I reeeeally don't want to have to do that!'

Amelia, Florence, Grimaldi and Tangine set off around the Fang Mansion on the hunt for the caticorns.

Squashy and Pumpy joined in the pursuit, pa-doinging and PA-DOOFING behind them, checking the nooks and crannies Amelia and her friends were too big to fit into. The two pumpkins sniffed around behind the cabinets, checked under the dressers and rolled into the deepest depths of Frivoleeta's many shoe closets. Pumpy, however, got distracted in the guest bathroom when he saw his own reflection in the toilet lid and began pouting at it lovingly.

'Pets really do resemble their owners,' Amelia muttered to herself.

The gang searched behind door after door, rummaged inside the cobweb-ridden kitchen cupboards (much to the disapproval of the cupboard trolls who were having a delightfully awful picnic); peered around every corner, explored shelf upon shelf, and even checked beneath the old fancy rugs.

'I can't find them anywhere!' said Tangine. 'I DID find a sad slug under the kitchen sink though. He said his name was Trevor and he is looking for his twin, Tina.'

Ameia was starting to think she really wasn't up to this big-sister business.

# CRASH!

'I FINK,' said Florence, 'THAT CAME FROM DIRECTLY ABOVE US.'

Amelia's cold heart fell into her toes. 'My bedroom is directly above us,' she said.

The friends sprinted up the spiral staircase and along the cavernous corridor, stopping dead outside Amelia's stripy bedroom door.

Giggles and meows rang out from behind it. Amelia swung the door open and was almost hit with a great big SPLAT of glittery paint in her face.

Mo cackled with laughter and carried on painting the wall with glitter paint.

Butler had stretched a pair of Amelia's stripy tights from one side of the room to the other. He now stood there in deep concentration plucking the taut material, making a satisfying *TWAAAAAAANG* each time.

Gerrard was dancing around the room with

the grace of a professional prancing yeti, which was very elegant indeed. He was holding one of Amelia's favourite ornaments – a delicate china pumpkin that her mum and dad had bought her for doing so well at Pumpkineers Club. He twizzled the precious object around, juggling it from one paw to the other.

'No, no, no! Put that down!' urged Amelia, trying to grab the shiny pumpkin.

But the little caticorn cleverly weaved his way around Amelia, dodging her swipes and hopping lightly on to a bookshelf. Amelia's large collection of POSITIVELY PUMPKIN magazines went tumbling to the floor, narrowly missing Squashy.

Mo lathered paint across the stripy wallpaper. Splodges of glitter were flying through the air as the artistic caticorn focused on her masterpiece.

Butler was still thrumming at the taut tights, with the musical *TWAAAAANG* getting louder and louder.

Amelia gasped as Gerrard dangled from the edge of the bookshelf with the pumpkin ornament precariously balanced in one of his paws.

'Gerrard. Listen to me!' said Amelia, beginning to lose her patience. 'If you don't get down from there *right now,* I'm going to have to tell Aunt Lavitora how naughty you've been. She won't be happy!'

But Gerrard wasn't listening. Whilst balancing on one paw, he slowly raised both back legs so that he was in a handstand position. He then tossed the pumpkin ornament up to his feet and, to Amelia's horror, began to juggle it!

Butler carried on thrumming at the tights.

THRUM THRUM TWAAAAAANG
THRUM THRUM TWAAAAAAAAAAANG

THRUM

THRUM

TWAAAAAAAAAAAAAAAANG!

Amelia's breathing got faster and shallower.

Gerrard continued juggling with his feet. The little model pumpkin bobbed around in the air like a tormented tangerine.

Amelia had had enough. She clenched her fists tightly and shouted at the top of her voice.

# 'STOP!'

Mo jumped in surprise. Her paintbrush soared through the air, spreading glitter across the ceiling, and landed with a SPLAT on Tangine's mop of white hair.

Tangine shrieked, causing Butler to twang the tights a bit too hard. They ripped, snapped and then smacked Florence right between the eyes.

And in amongst all of the chaos, Gerrard got his paws in a twist, and the little pumpkin ornament tumbled to the floor with a very definite . . .

# SMASH.

# CHAPTER 7

# WORN OUT AND HOPELESS

Amelia stood in the middle of her bedroom, staring at the shiny orange fragments scattered across the glitter-speckled floor.

'Amelia?' asked Grimaldi, touching her arm gently.

'I can't believe it,' Amelia said quietly, picking up a piece. 'This wasn't just any old ornament. It was special.'

'MAYBE WE COULD TRY FIXIN' IT FOR YOU?' suggested Florence.

'I'm quite good at fixing things,' said Grimaldi. 'I've had to glue my scythe together enough times!'

'I don't know,' said Amelia sadly. 'It looks pretty broken to me.'

Gerrard, Butler and Mo sniffed and whimpered.

'I DON'T KNOW WHY YOU'RE SNIFFLIN'. THIS IS ALL YOUR FAULT!' said Florence with a frown.

Gerrard started to cry.

'It's okay, Florence,' said Amelia.

'BUT THEY WERE BEING REALLY NAUGHTY,' said Florence. 'AND NOW THEY'VE RUINED ONE OF YOUR SUPER SPECIAL FINGS!'

'Florence does have a point,' Grimaldi agreed.

'I know,' said Amelia.

Tangine shuffled awkwardly in the bedroom doorway. He was twiddling his thumbs. 'I think that we should all go downstairs and calm down a bit.'

Florence furrowed her eyebrows and reluctantly nodded. 'FINE,' she said.

Amelia and Grimaldi ushered the caticorns downstairs to the unliving room, where the friends sat on the sofa feeling worn out and hopeless.

''ERE,' said Florence, tossing Unicornelius Pine in the direction of the caticorns. 'PLAY WIV YOUR EXPENSIVE TOYS AND FINK ABOUT WHAT YOU'VE DONE.'

'I think perhaps . . .' Tangine began, then hesitated.

'WHAT?' said Florence.

Tangine made a face. Amelia noticed he looked kind of sad. 'Never mind,' he said, quietly fiddling with his sleeve.

'I'm going to pop to the kitchen to make us some warm sour milk,' said Amelia. 'It might help everyone to relax.'

'Need a hand?' asked Grimaldi.

'No thank you,' said Amelia quietly. 'I won't be long.' She managed a small smile.

In the kitchen, Wooo was well on his way to being fully defrosted. His top half was in normal transparent ghost form, but his bottom half still resembled a gooey, ghostly puddle. He'd also managed to slide his way out of the jar.

'Hi, Wooo,' said Amelia, pulling out a chair and sitting down.

'You seem glum,' said the ghost butler.

Amelia let out a long sigh. She could feel a lump rising in her throat. 'The caticorns ran riot and ended up smashing my favourite pumpkin ornament,' she said. 'I lost my temper, and now they're really upset.'

'Little ones can be a challenge sometimes,' said Wooo. 'But you're doing your very best.'

'Wooo, I don't think I'm ready to be a big sister yet,' Amelia said suddenly. 'What if the

caticorns are being naughty because they don't like me? What if my own baby brother or sister doesn't like me?'

'Well, that's a preposterous thought,' said Wooo kindly.

Amelia found the words tumbling out of her mouth. 'I wanted to prove that I could be a responsible big sister so that Mum and Dad would be proud of me,' she said in a wobbly voice. 'But the house is a complete mess and the caticorns probably hate me for shouting at them. I didn't mean to. I just . . . I just . . .' Amelia's voice broke and she began to cry.

'Oh, Amelia,' said Wooo. 'Please don't be upset. There will be tricky times as your new baby brother or sister grows up, and some nights will be harder than others. But that's all part of being a big sister. You'll figure it out, I promise.'

It was at times like this that Amelia really

wished you could hug a ghost. She also wished Wooo wasn't still half-puddle.

'Thank you, Wooo,' she said, feeling a bit better. 'I should probably warm up the sour milk and get back to the unliving room, before the caticorns embark on another *smashing* adventure!'

'Oh, hoo hoo!' Wooo chortled. 'I see what you did there.'

# CHAPTER 8

# ATTENTION

As Amelia walked into the unliving room, she thought something odd had happened to her ears. She couldn't hear a thing. But then she realised why.

The caticorns were snuggled up together in the empty suitcase that had once been full of new expensive toys.

'SHHHHH, THEY FELL ASLEEP!' Florence said, as quietly as she could.

'It's a miracle!' whispered a relieved-looking Grimaldi.

Tangine was still sitting on the sofa in deep thought.

Amelia tiptoed over to her friends and handed out the glasses of sour milk before snuggling up next to Tangine. She took a long sip of the warm, soothing drink.

'Looking at the caticorns now, they seem so cute,' she said quietly. 'You'd never believe they could cause so much trouble!'

'They've worn themselves out after all that dancing, music and painting,' said Grimaldi.

'YOUR AUNT LEFT ALL THOSE PRESENTS FOR 'EM AND THEY STILL WEREN'T SATISFIED,' said Florence in disbelief. 'SHE SAID THE PRESENTS WOULD KEEP 'EM HAPPY! WHAT MORE COULD THEY POSSIBLY WANT?'

Tangine cleared his throat. 'Attention,' he said.

'Huh?' said Amelia.

'*Attention*,' Tangine repeated, more firmly this time.

'But we've given them attention,' said Amelia, feeling more confused than ever.

'Not in the way they *really* need it,' said Tangine. 'I suspect your Aunt Lavitora gives them lots of gifts to try to keep them happy.'

'"*Here's a suitcase filled with some gifts to keep them happy*",' Amelia quoted. 'That's exactly what my aunt said before she left.'

Tangine looked sad. 'Yes. Well, that's why I used to act like such a spoilt sprout, remember?'

Amelia did remember. When she had first met Tangine he was VERY different to the friendly, kind vampire-fairy she knew now. He had been bossy and spoilt and certainly didn't know how to act like a good friend.

'My dad thought that giving me presents all the time made up for the fact that he was never around when he was away searching for my mum. I had more expensive gifts than I could count,' said Tangine. 'But I didn't really *care* about the presents. All I REALLY wanted was to spend some time with my dad and for some friends – like you guys!'

'You're right, Tangine!' said Amelia. It was as if a lightbulb had flickered to life inside her head. 'In fact, so were *you*, Grimaldi!'

'Oh . . . okay?' said a blushing Grimaldi. 'But *how* was I right exactly?'

'"*They've worn themselves out after all that dancing, music and painting*" is what you said, Grimaldi,' explained Amelia, sitting up straight.

Grimaldi look at Amelia with a baffled expression.

'Guys, I've realised something,' said Amelia. She beckoned Florence, Grimaldi and Tangine to lean in closer. 'Gerrard is always dancing or swinging around on furniture. Butler is forever banging or tapping or plucking things to make music; and Mo is always drawing or painting on anything she can draw or paint ON!'

'INCLUDING OUR FACES,' Florence grunted.

'Don't you see?' said Amelia. 'They each have something special . . . a *unique* talent. But what if nobody has ever taken the time to notice it?'

'IT'S KINDA HARD TO APPRECIATE THEIR SKILLS WHEN THEY'RE RUNNIN' RINGS AROUND US,' said Florence.

'I know,' said Amelia. 'I think they just need us to take an interest in what they're doing instead of telling them off for it.' She smiled at her friends, giving Tangine a special wink. 'And I know exactly what we can do!'

The clock struck midnight and the caticorns began to stir. Gerrard gave a long squeaky yawn and slowly opened his eyes.

'You're up!' said Amelia happily.

Gerrard looked at her, clearly confused.

Butler and Mo stirred and opened their sleepy eyes. When they saw Amelia, they looked down at their paws guiltily.

'Come on! Up we get!' said Amelia enthusiastically. 'We have a surprise for you!'

Gerrard, Butler and Mo looked at each

other with wrinkled, furry little foreheads.

'Mew?' they said in unison.

Amelia whistled. Squashy and Pumpy came bundling into the unliving room wearing tiny top hats and bow ties.

'Squashy and Pumpy have been rather bored,' said Amelia, putting her hands on her hips. 'They need *entertaining*! And I thought to myself, I know JUST the trio who might be able to do that!'

Gerrard screwed up his little face in complete bafflement.

'We need someone who can DANCE!' declared Amelia. 'Now I wonder WHO around here can dance?'

Butler and Mo poked at Gerrard's head. 'Mew, mew, mew!' they chorused.

Gerrard stood up meekly and slowly twirled on the spot.

Amelia made an overly animated gasp. 'OH MY!' she said. 'You *can* dance!'

Gerrard nodded enthusiastically.

'Well then,' said Amelia. 'I'd best get Florence in here, so YOU can teach her some of your BEST dance moves for the show!'

'Mew?!' the caticorns echoed.

'THAT'S RIGHT,' said Florence, prancing into the room wearing a tutu and ballet slippers. 'THE SHOW!'

'We're going to put on a show together!' Amelia chimed. 'We can practise in front of Pumpy and Squashy, our very friendly judges, and then we can perform in front of Wooo and Aunt Lavitora. I bet she'll be so excited when she sees all the amazing things her caticorns can do!'

The caticorns were silent. They seemed stunned for a minute. Then, slowly but surely, the biggest smiles appeared on their adorable, fluffy little faces.

# CHAPTER 9
# IS SOMETHING DYING?

'Okay, we have our dancers!' said Amelia as Florence helped Gerrard pull on a ballet tutu and dance shoes. 'But our dancers need something to dance along to . . . Perhaps some music?'

Butler's ears pricked up.

'But I'm wondering WHO can play some beautiful music?' said Amelia, pretending to look puzzled.

Butler began jumping up and down on the spot.

'Oh! Of course! Butler!' said Amelia. Then she called towards the door. 'Come on in, guys!'

Grimaldi waltzed into the unliving room wearing a bow tie and a very TALL top hat. He was using his scythe as a conductor's stick.

'Let us make fangtastique muuuuuseeeeque!' sang Grimaldi in an overly posh voice.

Behind Grimaldi, making the most elaborate entrance so far, was Tangine, who'd borrowed a few things from Countess Frivoleeta's dressing room. He was wearing a long, frilly ballgown and on his head perched a tall, purple wig. His cheeks were covered in round splodges of red blusher.

'*Say hellooooooooo to your favourite operrraaaaaaaaaaa siiiiingeeeeeeeeeeer!*' Tangine sang, rolling his r's and over-pronouncing every syllable. 'Butler, my darrrrrrrling,' he trilled. 'TEACH ME!'

Butler giggled and meowed joyfully.

'You'd better get practising!' said Amelia. Then she leaned in and winked. 'Especially since Tangine will need ALL the training he can get!' Butler giggled even more.

Mo was left sitting cross-legged in the suitcase. She adjusted her glasses and twisted her tail around her paws.

Amelia settled herself down inside the suitcase with Mo and pulled out a sketchbook and a pencil from her skirt pocket. 'Mo, I do believe we have a whole STAGE SET to design!' said Amelia.

Mo's eyes grew wide. 'Mew mew?'

'Yep!' said Amelia. 'And I can't think of anyone better to paint it than you. With skills like yours, we're going to create the most beautiful scenery anyone ever laid eyes upon.'

Mo squeaked happily. Amelia passed her the pencil and opened the sketchbook to a blank page. 'Let's get to work!' she said.

It wasn't until the clock struck two in the morning that Amelia realised how absorbed they had all been. She was having so much fun with the caticorns and her friends, that she'd completely forgotten about lunch!

'I think it's time you filled your creative bellies,' said a friendly and familiar voice.

It was Wooo! He was finally fully defrosted. He was also carrying a HUGE plate full of tongue-twister sandwiches – Amelia's favourite!

'Looks like you worked things out,' he whispered as Amelia took a sandwich for herself and another for Squashy.

Amelia smiled. 'Look, Wooo! Look at the beautiful stage set Mo has been painting. And can you hear the *fangtastic* music Butler has composed? And check out the brilliant dance moves Gerrard has been teaching Florence.'

'FAAAAAAAAAAAR LAAAAR LAAAAAAAR!'

Pumpy rolled upside down and Squashy yelped in fright.

Wooo grimaced. 'What was *that*?' he asked. 'Is something dying?'

'That . . .' said Amelia in a hushed voice, 'is Tangine.' She raised an eyebrow. 'Need I say more?'

Wooo and Amelia looked at each other and burst out laughing.

Tangine came strutting towards the sandwich platter, clip-clopping in a pair of

Countess Frivoleeta's high-heeled shoes. 'I think I've got the hang of this opera malarkey,' he said airily. 'Another one to add to my list of never-ending talents.'

'Of course,' said Wooo, his expression unchanging. Amelia giggled. 'But in all seriousness,' Wooo added as Tangine sauntered away. 'We should all take a leaf out of Tangine's book. We all need to love ourselves a bit more. Including you, Amelia.'

A *BRIIIING! BRIIIING!* rang out from the hallway. 'I should get that,' said Wooo. He smiled and floated away.

Amelia grinned to herself as she watched her best friends in the entire world having fun with the caticorns. Soon she'd be able to do all of this with her new baby brother or sister! The uneasy feeling that had been nagging at her was finally starting to fade.

Had the baby been born yet? she wondered.

When would her mum and dad be home? She couldn't wait to introduce her new baby brother or sister to her world and her friends.

Gerrard, Butler and Mo bundled up to Amelia and began tugging at her skirt. 'Mew, mew, mew!' they chanted.

'You're all ready?' Amelia asked.

The caticorns nodded enthusiastically.

'Great!' said Amelia, feeling her tummy spin with excitement. 'Why don't the three of you get ready in the dining room. I'll fetch Wooo and we can rehearse the show. Then we'll be ready to do the real thing for Aunt Lavitora when she comes to pick you up.'

Amelia skipped to the kitchen where Wooo was preparing some sweet and salty snotcorn for the friends to munch on.

'Young Amelia! I have some good news,' he said with a big smile. 'That was your mum and dad on the phone. They will be back home by moonset.'

Amelia did a little excitable dance on the spot.

'Eeeeeeeeeeee, *I can't wait*!' she cried. 'Is Mum okay? Is it a baby boy or girl? How big is it? Does it look like me?!' Amelia thought she might explode with all the questions she had.

Wooo chuckled lightly. 'Everyone's fine and I am under strict instructions not to tell you anything more,' he said with a wink. 'BUT I do believe there's a fangtastic show rehearsal about to start, and I'm sure that'll keep your mind occupied for the rest of the night until they get home.'

'Okaaay,' said Amelia, pretending to look sad. But then she burst out laughing, hardly able to contain her joy. 'I'm just so excited! But you're right, Wooo, the show IS about to start. Would you like to come and watch with Squashy and Pumpy?'

'I'd love that,' said Wooo.

When Amelia and Wooo returned to the unliving room, Pumpy and Squashy were waiting patiently on the sofa, sporting monocles for ultimate observing and judging. Florence was poised in the centre of the stage set, which had been beautifully created to look like the Meadow of Loveliness in the Kingdom of the Light. Grimaldi waved his baton at the side of the set, in preparation for some serious conducting, and Tangine hid himself behind the unliving-room curtain whilst he warmed up his singing voice. 'EEEEEE EEEEEE OOOOOO OOOOOOOO AAAAAAAAA!' he sang, very loudly and VERY badly.

Amelia and Wooo snuggled up on the sofa next to the pumpkins with a big bowl of sweet and salty snotcorn.

'The caticorns are just getting ready in the dining room,' said Amelia. 'They'll be here in a minute!'

Minutes passed and Florence was still poised centre stage on one foot. Alone.

'THIS IS GETTING UNCOMFORTABLE,' she said, through gritted teeth.

'Maybe they've got stage fright?' wondered

Amelia. 'I'll go check if they're okay.'

But when Amelia entered the dining room, Gerrard's ballet shoes were sitting neatly on the table, Butler's homemade xylophone was perched on a chair, and Mo's sketchbook was

on the floor. There was no sign of the caticorns anywhere.

Florence pranced into the room behind Amelia. 'ME TOES WENT NUMB, SO I FORT I'D COME SEE WHAT WAS GOIN' ON.'

She hurrumphed when she saw that the caticorns weren't there. 'WHERE ARE THEY?'

Something on the other side of the large window caught Amelia's eye. Three little caticorns, pedalling away on a penny-farthing across the misty hills of Nocturnia.

# CHAPTER 10

# NOBODY EVER ASKED

'THE SHOW MUST GO OOOOOOOON!' Tangine's melodramatic tones resounded from behind the curtain in the unliving room.

'NO, YA BIG NOGGIN!' said Florence, marching into the room. She poked at the lump in the curtain so that Tangine's big purple wig toppled sideways into view. 'THE SHOW AIN'T GOIN' NOWHERE COZ THOSE LITTLE TRICKSTERS 'AVE RUN OFF AGAIN!'

Tangine's rosy-cheeked face suddenly appeared. '*What?!*' he said. 'So, I've been wasting my precious voice here?'

Amelia felt numb.

'I thought they'd changed,' she said to her friends. 'I . . . I thought . . . I think . . . *I don't know what I think any more!*' She put her head in her hands in despair. 'I AM SO CONFUSED!'

Grimaldi put an arm around Amelia.

Amelia suddenly felt her heart freeze over. 'Mum and Dad are going to be home soon and so will Aunt Lavitora! We HAVE to go after the caticorns.' She sighed. 'No matter how naughty or how mischievous they are, they can't be out there all on their own. They're just little creatures at the end of the night.'

'BUT 'OW ARE WE MEANT TO CATCH 'EM UP?' asked Florence. 'THEY'RE RIDING A PENNY-FARVING!'

'Has anyone actually considered where on earth they got a penny-farthing from?' asked Grimaldi.

But Amelia was too distracted to listen. She wracked her brain. It felt like a curly-wurly mess and she couldn't think straight.

Luckily Wooo floated in.

'Follow me!' he said.

Amelia, Florence, Grimaldi and Tangine braced themselves for the ride of a lifetime as Wooo revved up his classic motorcycle.

'How come we NEVER knew you had a *motorcycle*?' said Amelia, completely and utterly shocked.

'Nobody ever asked, young Amelia,' Wooo said with a wink.

The friends squeezed themselves into the motorcycle sidecar. Squashy and Pumpy managed to bag the main seat behind Wooo. And somehow, Wooo had enough helmets for all of them to wear.

''OW COME YOU 'AVE SO MANY 'ELMETS?' asked Florence when he handed her a large helmet with spots all over it.

'I make custom helmets as a hobby,' said Wooo with a smile. His own helmet was shaped like a larger version of his top hat.

Amelia wore a black helmet with a cobweb veil. Grimaldi's looked like a gnome's hat complete with a piece shaped like a beard that wrapped around his chin. Tangine, as usual, had picked the most extravagant and ridiculous helmet he could find. It was shaped like the tallest crown Amelia had ever set eyes upon, with flashing lights on each of the crown's points. But what made it look even more ridiculous was the fact that Tangine wore it on TOP of his big purple wig.

Squashy and Pumpy wore helmets that looked like their own pumpkin-shaped heads with round holes in the top for their stalks to poke through.

'Are you all ready?' asked Wooo as the exhaust coughed and spluttered plumes of thick black smoke.

'I WAS BORN READY!' said Florence, looking determined.

'I was never born ready for this,' said Grimaldi, gripping the sides of the tiny cart.

'Is this going to mess up my hair?' asked Tangine.

'Let's go!' said Amelia.

The motorcycle zoomed over the hills of Nocturnia so that the cold night air whipped at Amelia's cheeks. The occasional bat narrowly dodged the oncoming motorcycle and the occasional toad did not.

Grimaldi's die-phone was in overdrive.

*DING*! SQUISHED TOAD ALERT

*DING*! SQUISHED TOAD ALERT

*DING*! SQUISHED TOAD ALERT

'*Galloping gooseberries*,' Grimaldi groaned. 'I'm going to have a squished-toad waiting list as long as my scythe at this rate.'

Wooo weaved in and out of the cobbled streets and through Central Nocturnia Graveyard past a wobbly zombie yoga class. The motorcycle then zipped along the banks of the River Styx where Grimaldi and his family lived in a long gothic barge, then swung round tree trunk after tree trunk through the Petrified Forest.

As they rode through the trees, Amelia swore some of the plants on the ground were moving almost as fast as they were! But the Petrified Forest was *full* of wild and peculiar things, and it was often best not to look too closely.

The motorcycle picked up speed and Wooo leaned forward, concentrating hard on driving.

*'Wooo?! How do you know where you're going?!'* Amelia called over the rumbling engine and rush of wind.

They burst out from the trees of the Petrified Forest on to a clear dusty road. Not taking his eyes off the path before them, Wooo replied, 'I'm following the tracks of the penny-farthing wheels.'

*'It's impossible to follow anything at this speed!'* said Tangine, holding on to his helmet as the motorcycle suddenly

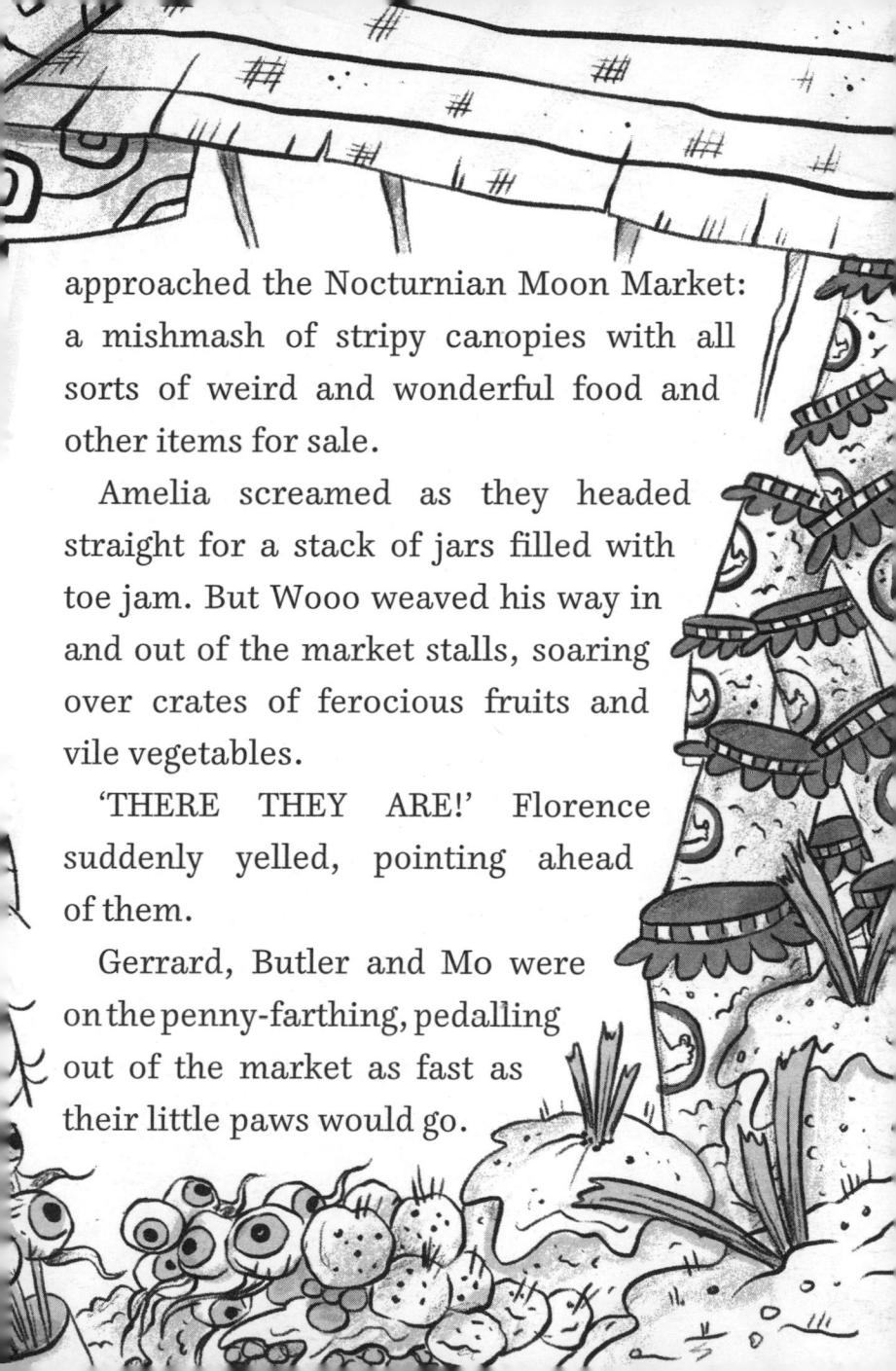

approached the Nocturnian Moon Market:
a mishmash of stripy canopies with all
sorts of weird and wonderful food and
other items for sale.

Amelia screamed as they headed
straight for a stack of jars filled with
toe jam. But Wooo weaved his way in
and out of the market stalls, soaring
over crates of ferocious fruits and
vile vegetables.

'THERE THEY ARE!' Florence
suddenly yelled, pointing ahead
of them.

Gerrard, Butler and Mo were
on the penny-farthing, pedalling
out of the market as fast as
their little paws would go.

'What are they up to?!' Grimaldi shrieked.

Wooo steered the bike out of the market, skidding and screeching as he handbrake-turned around a sharp corner on to the main dirt path through the Rickety Residences. This was one of the fanciest estates in Nocturnia, home to celebrities like the Howling Wolf band or the famous fashion designer Giorgio Arm an' Knee.

'GERRARD, BUTLER, MO!' Amelia shouted at the top of her voice. But the caticorns were too far away to hear her and the motorcycle engine was too loud. Wooo's wheels splattered thick mud on to the windows of the houses as they sped through the Rickety Residences.

The caticorns had gone full circle and they were all now headed back towards the Petrified Forest.

'WAAAAAAAIT!' Amelia called out.

'WE JUST WENT FRU 'ERE!' bellowed

Florence. 'I FINK THE CATICORNS MIGHT BE A BIT LOST!'

'That's why we have to catch up with them!' shrieked Amelia. 'They're probably scared to death!'

'Not "*to death*" I hope,' said Grimaldi. 'I have enough toads to be dealing with!'

Tangine made a strange noise. 'FLAAAAARG!' he cried out before coughing and spluttering. '*I think I just swallowed a dung beetle!*'

Wooo followed the frantically pedalling caticorns back towards the looming dark silhouette of the Petrified Forest. Amelia and the gang had almost caught up with them! The caticorns' little tails were tantalisingly close, and Amelia wondered, if she just leaned forward, she could almost –

Screeeeeeeeeech!

BOSH!

Wooo slammed on the brakes as the motorcycle crashed into the most enormous prickly bush.

'WHAT THE BATS?!' came Florence's muffled voice. She was head first in a tall verge of strange wiggly brambles that loomed high above them.

Amelia was close by, wedged in bum first along with Grimaldi, Tangine and the pumpkins.

'Is everyone okay?' Wooo asked, floating over to each of the friends in turn.

'Yes, I think so,' said Amelia, brushing herself down. 'What just happened?! The caticorns definitely went this way. But surely they would have bumped into the bushes too?' She carried on searching through the leaves in case they were buried inside somewhere.

Wooo looked worried.

'Hmmm,' he pondered, staring up at the hedge. 'You are right. The caticorns did head this way . . .' He looked around. 'And they most likely HAD a clear path.'

'I'M CONFUSED,' said Florence, easing herself out of the shrubbery. 'YOU'RE SAYIN' THE CATICORNS RODE FRU 'ERE FREELY, BUT WE CAN'T . . .'

'I'm confused too,' agreed Grimaldi.

Tangine adjusted his crown helmet. 'Sorry,

I didn't *actually* see what happened. I was too busy admiring how awesome my reflection looked in the back of Amelia's helmet.' He struck a pose. 'I mean, LOOK AT ME.' He was still wearing the ballgown and high heels.

'We can admire you later, Tangine,' said Amelia. 'Right now we have to find the caticorns!'

'We should probably move away from the bush,' urged Wooo, still looking concerned.

Suddenly there was a low rumbling sound. The branches began to wriggle and move around. The bush then started to change shape, creating a barrier around Amelia and her friends. A brand-new wall of wiggly plants formed where there hadn't been one before. Amelia's heart sank. They were trapped!

'Whaaaat . . . just happened?' asked Grimaldi nervously.

'I thought as much,' said Wooo. 'But I hoped

I was wrong.'

'Wooo? What's going on?' said Amelia, moving nearer to him for comfort. 'How is the bush moving around us?'

'This is no ordinary bush,' said Wooo. He took a closer look at one of the wiggling branches. 'I've studied a lot of plants in my time, and this looks just like Wiggleroot.'

'What's *Wiggleroot*?!' asked Amelia, unsure whether she actually wanted to know the answer.

'If my memory serves me correct,' said Wooo, 'it's a pesky plant that grows anywhere it wants, *whenever* it wants. It's extremely fast-growing, and develops into a labyrinth that doesn't stop changing.'

'A MOVIN' MAZE?' said Florence. 'THAT AIN'T GOOD.'

'That's not all,' said Wooo. He gulped.

'What's the matter?' Amelia asked.

Wooo adjusted his monocle. 'Anything or anyone trapped inside its maze, eventually gets . . . eaten.'

# CHAPTER 11

# I HATE WIGGLEROOT!

'*WHAT?!*' said Amelia, Florence, Grimaldi and Tangine all at once.

'SO, YOU'RE SAYIN', WE'RE TRAPPED INSIDE A PLANT THAT WILL EVENTUALLY EAT US?'

'To put it simply . . . yes,' said Wooo.

The friends began to clamber up the sides of the tall bush, but it was no use. Tangine tried to fly and Grimaldi tried to float over the wall of wiggling plants; but the higher they rose, the higher the Wiggleroot grew, as if it knew they were trying to escape.

'AARGH! It's no good!' shrieked Amelia.

'What are we going to DO? The caticorns are trapped in here somewhere too. We have to find them! I was meant to be *responsible* for them, and now they're about to get EATEN!'

'We're ALL about to get eaten!' said Grimaldi, hugging his scythe tightly.

'I'm FAR too beautiful to be consumed!' cried Tangine.

'I'm the only one who can pass through the walls of Wiggleroot,' said Wooo. 'So, I'll go and find help as quick as I can!'

'Okay. We'll hunt for the caticorns while you search for help,' said Amelia firmly.

'Keep moving and try not to stay in one place for too long. That's how the Wiggleroot gets you!' said Wooo, and he disappeared through the leaves.

The Wiggleroot began to stir.

'Collect the pumpkins. We'd better get going,' said Amelia, picking up Squashy and hugging him to her chest. 'Quick! This way!' she said, following a clear path in front of her.

Tangine tried to pick up Pumpy, but didn't have much luck. *'Why must you work out so much, Pumpy?!'* he said, straining to lift the heavy vegetable. 'Why can't you just be small like Squashy?!'

'I'LL TAKE 'IM!' said Florence, scooping Pumpy up as if he were as light as a feather. 'LET'S GO!'

Amelia, Florence, Grimaldi and Tangine hurtled down a clear route between the bushes.

'OOOF!' Florence, who had been leading the charge, suddenly bounced backwards and landed on her bottom with a thud. 'IT'S ALWITE, I STILL GOT YOU, PUMPY!' she declared, looking quite proud.

The walls of the maze had twisted and transformed around them, blocking their way again. Amelia hadn't even noticed it happen this time.

The others skidded to a halt. Amelia and Tangine reached down to help Florence up.

'What shall we do now?' asked Amelia, feeling slightly desperate.

'This way?' suggested Grimaldi, pointing down the new and only clear path with his scythe.

Everyone turned around, running until they approached a crossroads.

'*Now what?*' asked Tangine, looking from side to side.

'I don't know,' said Amelia. 'GERRARD? BUTLER? MO? *Where are youuuuu?!*' she called out as loud as she could.

'Meeeeeeeeew!'

Amelia whipped around. 'GERRARD?! BUTLER?! MO?!' she shouted even louder. 'WE'RE HERE! KEEP MEOWING SO WE CAN

FOLLOW THE SOUND!'

'Meeeeeew! Meeeeeew! Meeeeeew!'

Amelia ran towards the distressed mews of the caticorns, and soon found herself face first with a tangle of Wiggleroot vines. A new bush quickly formed in front of her.

'I HATE WIGGLEROOT!' she yelled, thrashing at the wriggling creepers.

'This is impossible!' said Tangine. 'The plants won't stop changing shape!'

'*Mew*?!'

'*Mew, mew*?!'

'I FINK THE CATICORNS MIGHT BE ON THE UVVA SIDE OF THIS HEDGE,' said Florence, pressing her ear against the wall of Wiggleroot.

Suddenly, the vines slithered and twisted around Pumpy, who was still nestled under Florence's arm.

'OI!' yelled Florence, trying to yank the

gripping plant off the bewildered pumpkin. But the more she tugged, the more the Wiggleroot wrapped around him and tightened its grip. Pumpy let out a distressed squeak.

Tangine came hurtling towards the hedge as fast as his high heels could carry him. He grabbed Grimaldi's scythe as he passed and swung it through the air.

'WATCH OUT, FLORENCE!' he yelled, a look of sheer determination and anger on his face. He lurched forward and screamed as loud as he could: 'GET AWAY FROM MY PUMPKIN, YOU BRANCH!'

He swiped at the Wiggleroot with Grimaldi's scythe, cutting it clean in half.

Pumpy went tumbling to the ground as the snake-like branches recoiled into the bush. The wall of plants pulsed and groaned, before beginning to twist and snarl and change shape once again.

'We'd better run before they try to eat one of us again!' said Amelia urgently.

Florence swept both Pumpy and Tangine up under one arm. The friends ran as fast as they could, away from the wall of branches.

Amelia's legs were beginning to ache as she sprinted through the labyrinth of Wiggleroot, turning corner after corner. The friends winged round one path and then another, then turned back on themselves. It felt as if they were running around in circles. Amelia had absolutely NO idea where the bats they – or the caticorns – were.

'GERRARD?! BUTLER?! MO?!' she called out again.

'*Meeeeeeeew*!'

Amelia stopped suddenly and listened.

'*Meeeeeeeeeeew*!'

'They're close!' she panted.

Amelia did a three-hundred-and-sixty degree turn and ran towards the distraught sounds of the little caticorns. She stumbled around a corner and tripped over something soft and fluffy, before tumbling face first into the mud. Squashy fell out of her arms, rolling across the ground. Grimaldi stumbled over Amelia, and Florence fell over Grimaldi, doing an ungraceful roly-poly across the dirt and landing on top of a very unfortunate Tangine and Pumpy.

Amelia spat out a mouthful of mud and looked up to see what she had tripped on.

'Gerrard!' she cried out with relief.

'Butler! Mo!'

'Meeeeeeeeeeeeeew!'

The little caticorns ran over to Amelia and, to her surprise, helped her to her feet. They looked scared.

'I'm so relieved you're all okay,' said Amelia. 'I was really worried about you!' She then sighed. 'Why the bats did you go running off like that?'

Something fell out of a small bag dangling from Gerrard's paw. Just before it dropped on to the muddy ground, Mo leaped forward and caught the object in her paws.

'What's that?' asked Amelia.

Mo stepped forward and opened her paws slowly.

Amelia gasped.

There was a little pumpkin ornament exactly like the one that had belonged to Amelia.

When she picked it up, she saw there

was a price tag dangling from it. It was
brand-new.

'You weren't running away, were you?'
she said.

Gerrard shook his head. Butler pointed at
the pumpkin. Mo gave Amelia a small,
regretful smile.

'Mew,' she said.

'Mew,' said Gerrard apologetically. He put

his paws around Amelia's waist, followed by Butler and Mo.

Amelia felt tears well up in her eyes. 'That's really *really* nice of you to buy this for me,' she said sincerely, and wrapped her arms around the three little creatures. 'Thank you.'

'UM, AMELIA,' said Florence, tapping her on the shoulder. 'YOU MIGHT WANNA SAVE THE EMOTIONAL MOMENT FOR LATER COZ, UM, WELL, WE'RE ABOUT TO GET EATEN BY A BUSH . . .'

## CHAPTER 12

# REST IN PEACE, BEAUTIFUL SHOE

Florence was right.

One of the Wiggleroot bushes had morphed into something far more than just a bush. Arms and legs made from long, twisted branches burst out from a thick torso of leaves and twigs.

At the very top of this shrubbery daymare were two gaping holes where its eyes should have been, and a large mouth that roared loudly, spluttering leaves and soil over the friends. The Wiggleroot monster rose up high in the air, before diving to the ground and slithering its way towards the gang.

'RUN!' Amelia shouted.

She picked up Squashy. Florence scooped up the three caticorns under one arm with Pumpy under the other. Tangine and Grimaldi followed close behind, with the Wiggleroot monster drawing ever closer. Its long, spindly branches warped and stretched, sliding across the forest floor, interlacing its snake-like roots around one of Tangine's heels.

'Aaaaaaargh!' Tangine shouted, almost falling over. At the very last moment, he just managed to slip his foot out of the trapped shoe, before it was swept away into the Wiggleroot monster's embrace. 'NOOOOO!' cried Tangine. 'Give that back!'

'JUST KEEP RUNNING, TANGINE! FORGET ABOUT THE SHOE!' bellowed Florence as their friend clambered to his feet.

'But . . . it was such a *pretty* shoe!' Tangine cried in anguish, before turning to the monster and yelling, 'and now my feet don't MATCH! How DARE you deny me THAT!'

Tangine began marching lopsidedly towards the Wiggleroot monster in a fury.

'Tangine, STOP!' yelled Amelia. *'What are you doing?!* You're going to get yourself eaten next!' She sprinted back towards an enraged Tangine and grabbed his arm. *'Come on!* This way!'

The monster spotted Amelia and Tangine and began to slither towards them. Fast.

'Meeeeeew!' yelled Gerrard.

'NOT NOW, GERRARD,' said Florence, clinging tightly to the little caticorn.

But Gerrard managed to squirm his way out of Florence's grip and began scampering straight towards the Wriggleroot monster looming over Amelia and Tangine.

In a split second Butler and Mo followed.

'STOOOOOOOOOP!' Amelia cried.

But everything seemed to move in

slow motion. Gerrard ran in front of her and Tangine, then began to cartwheel and pirouette his way around the approaching Wiggleroot monster, making the huge beast twist round and round, upside down and loop the loop so much that it looked positively dizzy.

Butler then cleared his throat and took in a deep breath.

'LA LA LA . . . LAAAAAAAAAAR!'

His voice was so high and so piercing that everyone had to cover their ears.

'There are too many things happening!' squeaked a confused and terrified Grimaldi.

It was all too much for the Wiggleroot monster. Finally it collapsed into a big tangle of vines. The surrounding bushes slunk back.

Mo was quick to act, taking handfuls of the crumpled Wiggleroot and tying it up into the most intricate knots Amelia had ever seen

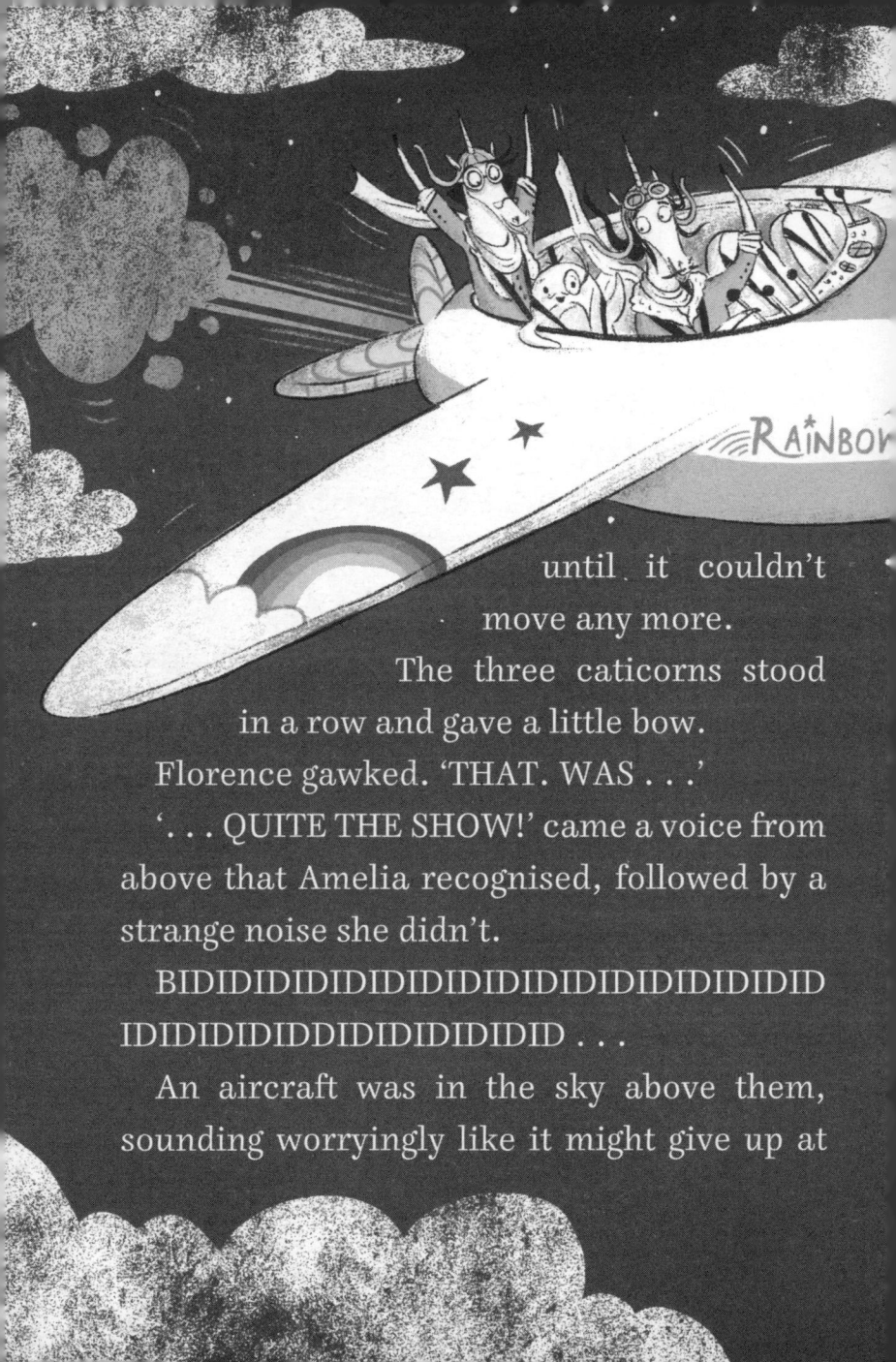

RAINBOW

until it couldn't
move any more.

The three caticorns stood
in a row and gave a little bow.

Florence gawked. 'THAT. WAS . . .'

'. . . QUITE THE SHOW!' came a voice from
above that Amelia recognised, followed by a
strange noise she didn't.

BIDIDIDIDIDIDIDIDIDIDIDIDIDIDIDID
IDIDIDIDIDDIDIDIDIDIDID . . .

An aircraft was in the sky above them,
sounding worryingly like it might give up at

any moment. But someone leaned over the edge and gave a big wave – and Amelia *definitely* recognised him.

'WOOO!'

'I found some help,' said Wooo with a big smile. Amelia was so relieved that she thought she might faint.

The 'help', who also happened to be the pilot, leaned over the edge and lifted his goggles.

It was a unicorn.

'RICKY!' cried Florence in delight.

Another unicorn popped up from the back of the plane.

'Graham!' said Grimaldi, waving his scythe happily up at the sky.

Amelia and her friends had met Ricky and Graham many times. The unicorn duo had been guards, detectives, mountain-safety experts and now, apparently, air rescue. They were unicorns of many talents and Amelia was very grateful that they always seemed to be there in times of need.

'*Watch yerselves!*' called Graham as he threw a thick rope out of the aircraft.

Amelia grabbed the rope. 'Got it!' she confirmed. 'Gerrard, Butler, Mo! You three climb up first!'

The caticorns obeyed, with Gerrard giving Amelia an affectionate lick on her cheek before the three little creatures scrambled up the rope into the safety of the aircraft. Ricky and Graham looked enchanted by their new fluffy aeroplane guests.

Tangine followed, with Grimaldi clambering up after him.

'Tangine, do you mind?!' Grimaldi yelped. 'Your high heel is IN my eye socket! Can't you take it off? You don't even have the *pair* any more.'

Tangine looked down towards Grimaldi and gave an offended gasp. 'Well, *maybe* your eye socket shouldn't be in the WAY of my shoe!' he snarked. 'And how dare you suggest I remove it? That's like telling YOU to remove your head!'

Florence climbed halfway up the rope and then reached out so that Amelia could throw Squashy up to her. Florence caught the little pumpkin in one hairy paw and expertly launched him into Graham's waiting hooves. Amelia tried to pick up Pumpy but hadn't realised *quite* how heavy he was.

'I can't lift Pumpy!' she called up to Florence in a panic.

Tangine, who had finally made it into the aircraft, leaned over the edge and yelled: 'PUMPY! DO THE THING!'

Pumpy waggled his stalk once with a look of sheer determination. Then with one huge PA-DOOOOOOOOOING he bounced towards the aeroplane, corkscrewing through the air like a round orange torpedo. He bounced high enough so that Florence was able to catch him with one arm and fling him up to safety.

Amelia was the last to climb up into the protection of Ricky and Graham's strange and tiny flying machine. She saw with some alarm that the Wriggleroot had unknotted itself and was on the move again.

'Don't worry,' said Ricky, adjusting his

flying goggles. 'We're gonna treat that Wiggleroot with some WIGGLIGONE first fing tomorrow. It will turn it into a nice plant that don't eat fings!'

Amelia smiled. She pulled Squashy and the caticorns into a big hug and let out a long sigh of relief. 'I'm so glad you're all safe,' she whispered.

The murky skies over the city of Nocturnia began to get lighter, creating a blood-red strip along the horizon, and the moon had almost disappeared.

'Ooh,' said Amelia, suddenly feeling excited. 'Mum and Dad will be home with my new brother or sister any time now! We'd better hurry back so I don't miss their arrival!'

'Meeeeeeeew!' sang the caticorns together.

'And we should get ready to perform your special show in front of Aunt Lavitora, who will be back soon,' Amelia added, ruffling each of the caticorns' furry heads. 'She's going to love it!'

Ricky put his foot down and the small aircraft chugged along a little bit faster, even under the weight of all its new occupants.

Pumpy suddenly made a very strange noise.

'Are you okay?' asked Amelia.

Pumpy went completely cross-eyed, then gave a massive BELCH. Out popped something shiny, diamond-studded, and shaped just like . . .

'MY SHOE!' Tangine squeaked with joy and picked up the slobbery item. 'How the BATS did you manage to get this?!' Then he paused. 'You know what, it doesn't matter.' He slipped the shoe on to his bare foot and waved it around before announcing proudly, 'IT FITS!'

# CHAPTER 13

# SAVED YOUR ROYAL BOTTOM

Ricky and Graham's aircraft landed with a THUD outside the Fang Mansion. John the Vulture was still collapsed in the yard, eating any slugs that trailed past within tongue-stretching distance.

As Amelia opened the door to the mansion, a *BONG* rang out from the grandfather clock in the entrance hall marking the hour.

'We'd better get this place cleaned up,' she said urgently. Amelia had forgotten how messy the house was. The caticorns' trail of destruction was everywhere. 'I need to show Mum and Dad that I AM a responsible big sister. If they see the house like this, they'll be so cross.'

'Young Amelia,' said Wooo, touching her shoulder gently. 'You've already shown your mum and dad what a brilliant big sister you are, and the baby will love you just as much as everyone here does. Just remember to always be *you*.'

Amelia smiled. She really, REALLY wished you could hug a ghost. She glanced at the glitter-stained walls and food splodges spread across the carpet.

'Well, I'd *still* really like to tidy up so that everything is just perfect for my new baby brother or sister!'

'We can help you clean up,' said Ricky. 'If you like?'

'That would be amazing, thank you!' said Amelia, grateful for her brilliant friends.

'Yeah, we've finished our first-ever flying

practice for the night,' said Graham. 'So we're as free as flamingo-dragons!'

'Wait,' said Tangine. 'You've *never* flown that thing before?'

'Nope,' said Ricky as he waltzed into the Fang Mansion and grabbed a cloth.

'I reckon we'll get the hang of it soon enough,' said Graham indifferently.

'We could have DIED,' said Tangine, marching in behind them. 'We could have crashed, and my beautiful face would have been ruined! You put the FUTURE KING of Nocturnia at RISK, don't you know?!'

The two unicorns stared at Tangine. Both raised their eyebrows.

'Mate, we just saved your royal bottom,' said Ricky. 'We *saved* THE FUTURE KING! I reckon we deserve some kind of royal medal for that. Don't you think so, Graham?'

'Good point, Ricky,' said Graham.

He smiled at Tangine. 'Let us know when the award ceremony is, and I'll wear my BEST hat.'

Tangine harrumphed.

Wooo grabbed a handful of cloths and mops from the cellar, and the friends got to work.

Squashy and Pumpy took care of the dining room, each brandishing a feather duster in their stalks and a cloth in their mouths. Pumpy had gone the extra mile by wearing an apron with a picture of a six-pack on it.

Florence scrubbed the glitter off the walls, whilst Grimaldi used his scythe to gather up all the broken bits of furniture, and Tangine made sure every vase was turned to face the right way.

The caticorns helped Amelia tidy up her bedroom so that it looked as good as new.

'Oh! One more thing!' said Amelia as they stood in the doorway, about to leave. She pulled the shiny little pumpkin ornament out of her skirt pocket and placed it on her bookshelf in place of the old one.

'Perfect!' She smiled and ruffled each of the caticorns' furry heads. They giggled and hugged Amelia tightly.

'I'm going to miss you guys,' Amelia said, suddenly feeling sad.

But she didn't have time to dwell any more, as the sounds of the door gong echoed through the mansion.

Amelia and the caticorns rushed into the entrance hall, followed by Wooo, her friends, and Ricky and Graham. Squashy and Pumpy were still wearing tiny aprons and holding feather dusters. Amelia braced herself for the arrival of the new baby.

But it wasn't her mum and dad at the door.

'FLOOFY WOOFY DOO-DAAAAAAHS!' sang the shrill voice of Aunt Lavitora.

The caticorns ran up to Aunt Lavitora and danced around her feet.

'Mew! Mew! Mew!' they sang.

Amelia chuckled, and announced, 'Aunt Lavitora, your caticorns have a special surprise for you.'

'Oh! Really?' said Lavitora. 'I do love surprises!'

'Mew! Mew-mew, mew!' said Gerrard happily.

'Meeeeew meeeew!' added Butler.

'MEW MEW!' finished Mo.

Aunt Lavitora gasped in response. 'An important show? Right here, right now?'

Amelia stepped forward and smiled at the caticorns. 'There is indeed! Aunt Lavitora, will you follow me?'

She took her aunt's silk-gloved hand and led her through to the unliving-room sofa. Mo's hand-painted scenery stood proudly in the centre of the room. Butler's handmade instruments were poised at the side of the stage, ready to make beautiful music.

'Darklings, what is going on?' asked Aunt Lavitora as Wooo placed a bowl of sweet and salty snotcorn on to her lap.

'Just make yourself comfy, Aunt Lavitora,'
Amelia said, grinning. 'Here goes . . .'

# CHAPTER 14

# USEFULCORNS

'Oooh, oooh!' said Ricky eagerly, 'Can me and Graham watch too?!'

'Of course!' said Amelia, ushering the unicorns into the unliving room. 'Come through and make yourselves at home!'

Ricky and Graham sat on the sofa either side of a very confused-looking Aunt Lavitora. She looked from Ricky to Graham before picking up a piece of snotcorn and asking, 'Who *are* you exactly?'

'We . . .' began Ricky, scooping a hoof-full of snotcorn into his mouth. He chewed and chewed some more. Aunt Lavitora waited. *MUNCH MUNCH MUNCH MUNCH . . .*

Graham shook his head and sighed.

'*He's* Ricky and *I'm* Graham and we are anything you want us to be, really.'

Ricky finally gulped down his mouthful of snotcorn. 'Yeah!' he said. 'We saved your caticorns from being eaten by a plant monster too. We are your ALL-ROUND-UNICORNS really. Useful unicorns.'

'USEFULCORNS!' Ricky and Graham blurted out at the same time, before high-hooving each other across Lavitora's face.

Aunt Lavitora looked from one unicorn to the other, then shrieked, 'My darkling caticorns were almost eaten by a *WHAT* monster?!'

Luckily, just at that moment, Wooo dimmed the lights and music started as the show began.

Squashy and Pumpy bounced on to each of the sofa arms still wearing their tiny aprons. They waved their feather dusters around with their stalks and squeaked gleefully as Amelia introduced the show.

'THIS is a special performance of the well-loved Nocturnian tale, *THE YETI WHO WANTED TO FLY*!' she said dramatically. 'We hope you enjoy our show!'

Ricky and Graham cheered, Aunt Lavitora clapped and the pumpkins squeaked as the music came to a glorious end.

Aunt Lavitora flounced on to the stage and embraced the caticorns. 'Oh, Gerrard, my precious little snot-globule, I never knew you could dance like that! And Butler, that music was divine. You are so talented, my darkling! As for this masterpiece,' Aunt Lavitora continued, stroking a picture of a pretty flower on the cardboard stage set. 'Well, Mo, I just don't have the words . . .'

'WELL, THAT'S A SHOCKER,' Florence muttered under her breath. Grimaldi tried to hold in a giggle, but ended up spraying snot all over his cloak.

Amelia's cold vampire heart swelled with pride at what the caticorns had achieved with a little bit of help from their friends. She was also relieved at how impressed Aunt Lavitora was with it all.

'Actually, one moment! I DO have some words after all!' Aunt Lavitora declared, beaming at Amelia and the others.

Florence raised an eyebrow. 'KNEW IT WAS TOO GOOD TO BE TRUE.'

Amelia looked around at her friends in excited anticipation of the praise to come.

'I do so hope that *one* delightfully dreadful night, you may ALL wake up and be as talented as my fluffy babies!' Aunt Lavitora trilled. 'You could learn a lot from them, you know. You really could!'

Amelia rolled her eyes but then laughed to
herself. Unlike the tiny caticorns, it seemed
Aunt Lavitora was never going to change.

Tangine, on the other hand, was having
none of it. His face had turned as purple as his
curly wig. 'HANG ON one royal second,' he
said. 'I think you'll find that THE—'

CREEEEEEEEEEEEEEAAAAAAAAK!

The sound of a door slowly opening came
from upstairs. Amelia looked up towards the
ceiling, then looked at Wooo.

'Amelia?' came the voice of Countess Frivoleeta.

Amelia felt like all of her limbs had gone numb and her heart began to beat faster.

This was it. Her parents were home.

Amelia rushed to the spiral staircase.

Countess Frivoleeta and Count Drake emerged at the top. Their eyes were tired but bright, and they had big fang-filled smiles on their faces.

Amelia rushed forward, then paused. In her mother's arms was a big bundle of shimmery black fabric.

'Is that . . . ?' Amelia whispered.

Her mother nodded and beckoned to Amelia.

Amelia walked over slowly. Her mother leaned forward gently.

And there he was.

'Meet Vincent Fang,' said the countess softly. 'Your new baby brother.'

# CHAPTER 15

# VINCENT

Until that moment, Amelia hadn't thought it possible to feel the amount of love she felt for her baby brother. It was as if the love was flooding through her cold veins and bursting out of her like a glitterbomb explosion.

'Vincent,' she said, stroking the tiny vampire's cheek. He was so small. But he had the same round face and tiny black freckles as Amelia.

'Would you like to hold him?' asked Countess Frivoleeta.

Amelia nodded.

Her mother placed Vincent carefully into Amelia's arms. He was much lighter than Squashy. The baby vampire began to stir, before slowly opening his big eyes.

Amelia felt a smile spread across her face, until she was grinning more than she'd ever grinned before!

'Hello, Vincent,' she said. It was as if nobody else was in the room. Just Amelia and her new little brother. 'We are going to have so much fun together.'

She knelt down and beckoned to Squashy. 'This is our pet pumpkin, Squashy,' she told Vincent. Squashy sniffed at the baby vampire's face and waggled his stalk from side to side happily.

'And these are my best friends in the entire world,' Amelia said, walking over to Florence, Grimaldi and Tangine, before whispering, 'Tangine doesn't *always* wear a big purple wig.' She looked at Tangine and winked.

'Well, Vincent Fang,' said Tangine. 'Your big sister is *quite* mistaken . . . It's PRINCE

Tangine La Floofle the First actually. And I'm *sure* those will be your first words.' Then he turned to Countess Frivoleeta and lifted a foot. 'How much would you accept for these shoes? I think I'm in love.'

Amelia's mother chuckled and put an arm around Tangine's shoulder. 'If you like them that much, they're *yours*, darkling!'

Tangine gasped and kissed Vincent on the cheek in sheer delight. 'You have the BEST mother, Vincent Fang!'

Vincent gurgled in Amelia's arms and then farted.

'BEST WAY TO RESPOND TO A PRINCE, I SAY!' said Florence.

'This is Wooo. He's the best ghost *ever*.' Amelia smiled at the wonderful ghost butler who had floated over. 'He will always make sure you believe in yourself no matter how hard things may seem.'

Wooo bowed his head and tipped his top hat.

'And here are the unforgettable Ricky and Graham!' said Amelia, turning to the two unicorns. 'They always seem to be there when you need them most.'

Ricky and Graham beamed and nodded their heads, accidentally cracking horns. 'OW!'

'They are USEFULCORNS!' Aunt Lavitora chipped in, looking proud of herself.

Ricky and Graham gave Aunt Lavitora a high-hoof. 'You nailed it!' Ricky cheered.

Aunt Lavitora gazed at Vincent and looked as if she might cry. She put one arm around the three caticorns and another around Amelia's shoulders.

'Look at how ickle he is,' Lavitora sniffed. 'You all used to be that small,' she told the caticorns.

Gerrard, Butler and Mo stared at Vincent, their eyes wide with fascination.

'Do you want a cuddle with him?' Amelia asked them. 'If you sit on the sofa nicely, I can put him between you all.'

The caticorns ran to the sofa, snuggling into the stripy velvet cushions. Amelia very carefully placed Vincent between them and the caticorns all put their paws around him. Aunt Lavitora began to sob, followed by Countess Frivoleeta.

'Oh my,' said Count Drake. 'There's a lot of emotion in this room right now.' He sniffed. 'And I'm feeling it too!'

Amelia, Florence, Grimaldi and Tangine shared a glance and giggled. Amelia leaned in towards Vincent and whispered, 'Our family is rather weird.' She stroked his little pale cheek. Vincent burped up a tiny splodge of sick. 'But I think you'll fit right in,' Amelia said with a grin.

'You know, Amelia,' said Aunt Lavitora. 'You're going to make such a wonderful big sister.'

Lavitora turned to the countess and smiled. Countess Frivoleeta almost choked in shock.

Count Drake leaned in to Amelia's mum and whispered, 'Are you SURE that's your *real* sister?'

'I, er, I . . . that's a lovely thing to say!' said Countess Frivoleeta, still stunned. 'I'd offer you some scream tea, but I'm guessing you have to shoot off?'

Aunt Lavitora raised an eyebrow. 'Frivvy dear, I'd love nothing more than to stay for a cup of scream tea.'

Countess Frivoleeta's eyes grew wide.

'Maybe I'll even stay for TWO,' Lavitora added casually.

And then both of Countess Frivoleeta's eyeballs popped out.

'Okey-dokey,' Wooo said to the room. 'How many for scream tea and tongue-twister sandwiches?!'

'MEEEEEEEEE!' shouted everyone, apart from Countess Frivoleeta, who had fainted.

'You're going to have so much fun with your little brother!' said Grimaldi as the friends prepared for a second showing of *THE YETI WHO WANTED TO FLY* (at Amelia's parents' request).

'I'm so excited!' said Amelia, who was still cuddling the baby vampire. 'There are so many things I want teach him. I don't know where to start!'

'YOU CAN TELL 'IM ALL ABOUT PUMPKINS,' said Florence, putting a big hairy arm around Amelia's shoulders.

'And blame him for stuff you did but don't want to get told off for,' said Tangine proudly.

Florence raised an eyebrow. 'NO, TANGINE, YOU DON'T DO THAT.'

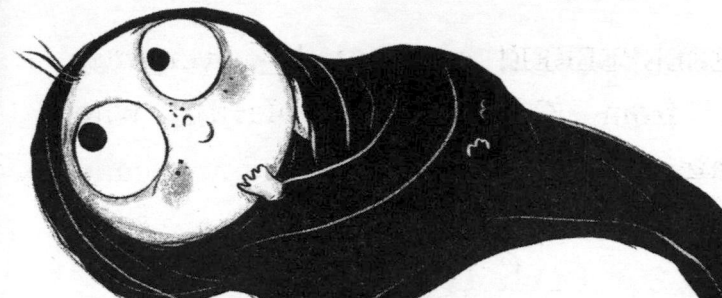

Tangine looked confused. 'Oh.' He scratched his head. 'Are you *sure*?'

The friends laughed.

Then a very unpleasant smell filled the air.

'Oh my!' shrieked Aunt Lavitora, squeezed on the sofa with Ricky, Graham, the count and countess. 'Drake, was that YOU?!'

Count Drake gasped and looked offended. 'How could you, Lavitora?!' he said defensively. 'You would KNOW if it were me. I think you'll find Vincent has successfully filled his first nappy!'

Everybody in the room covered their noses. Count Drake looked over to Amelia, who was grimacing. 'Well, Amelia, my awful little onion skin,' he said. 'I feel like this is a job for Vincent's *fangtastic* big sister!'

Amelia flared her nostrils. She'd not really thought about the smelly part of having a baby brother! But she didn't mind.

'Well, I'd better get you cleaned up before the show starts,' she told Vincent. 'You're one stinky little vampire. But I love you very, VERY much.'

Vincent made a gurgling sound and smiled.

'I think he likes me!' Amelia said to her mum and dad.

The countess chuckled. 'He doesn't *like* you,' she said simply.

Amelia looked at her mum with a puzzled expression.

Countess Frivoleeta kissed Amelia on the cheek and gave her a gentle squeeze.

'He *loves* you. Just like we all do!'

# THE END

# Make a Batty Bookmark!

These bookmarks sit perfectly in the corner of the page. You can decorate them to look like your favourite characters!

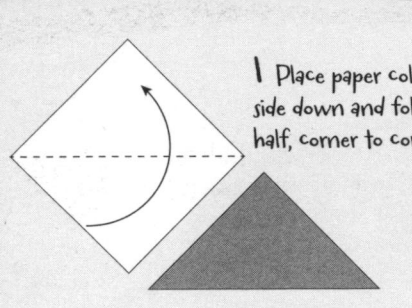

1 Place paper coloured side down and fold in half, corner to corner

2 Fold top down to meet bottom edge

3 Fold each bottom point in to meet at the middle, then open out again.

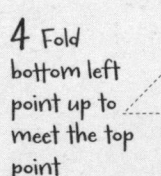

4 Fold bottom left point up to meet the top point

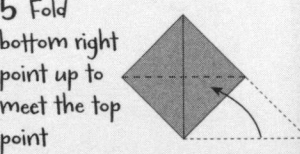

5 Fold bottom right point up to meet the top point

*Be careful using scissors.
Ask an adult if you need help.

# You will need

- Paper that is coloured on one side (wrapping paper is perfect!) — 17cm square
- Scraps of coloured paper
- Coloured pens
- Glue
- Scissors*

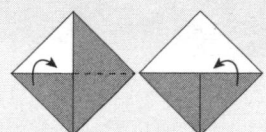

**6** Along the folds, tuck the top parts of the triangles inside

**7** Tuck the top triangle inside

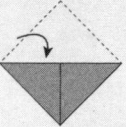

**8** Using your paper scraps, cut out 2 wings, 2 fangs and 2 eyes.

**9** Glue on the wings, fangs and eyes, to make the battiest bat bookmark!

Why not make your favourite character or create your own ghoul?

# Amelia Fang Character Quiz

## Which Amelia Fang character are YOU most like?

On a trip to the fairy-ground, which snack would you choose?

a. Cuddly Custard Pies
b. Fairy Floss
c. Tongue-Twister Sandwiches
d. Strawberry Sherbet Shake

Your favourite fairy tale is...

a. Beauty and the Beast
b. The Frog Prince
c. Jack and the Beanstalk
d. The Emperor's New Clothes

Your favourite hobby is...

a. Keeping fit
b. Drawing pictures of your best yeti and fairy friends
c. Playing with your pet and hanging out with your friends
d. Watching the Great Gothic Gravestone Carve Off

If you could have one superpower, what would it be?

a. Super strength
b. Invisibility
c. Flight
d. Super speed

Your favourite colour is...

a. White
b. Black
c. Orange
d. Purple

Your bedroom is...

a. Very messy, but you know where everything is
b. Very tidy, you like things in their right places
c. A bit messy, sometimes you don't have time to tidy up all your books
d. Quite tidy, you need space for your pet pumkin to bounce around, right?

When confronted by danger, do you...

a. Charge in, you're not afraid of anyone or anything!
b. Worry and panic a bit, but then make sure you're there to help your friends.
c. Consider all the options and then make a plan.
d. See if there's a mummy maid around to help, and then remember that your friends need you and you would never let them down!

## MOSTLY As
### You're like FLORENCE
Brave, strong and certain to make an impression!

## MOSTLY Bs
### You're like GRIMALDI
You may sometimes be a bit of a worrier, but you're always there for your friends.

## MOSTLY Cs
### You're like AMELIA
You're a real leader and a great friend.

## MOSTLY Ds
### You're like TANGINE
Fun and loyal, but you do like a bit of luxury in your life!

# AMELIA FANG

Join the little
vampire with a big heart
for some howlingly hilarious adventures!

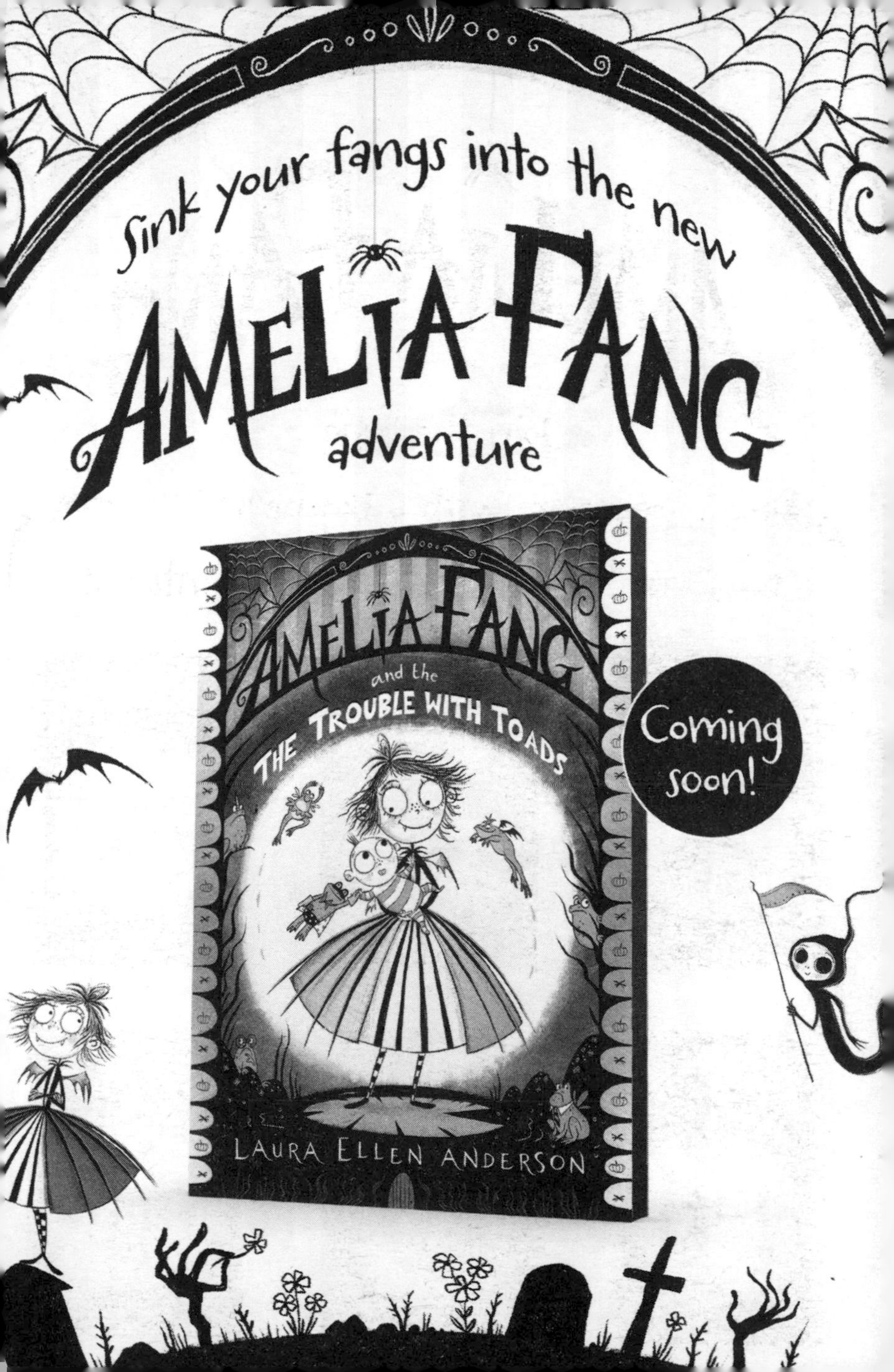

Sink your fangs into the new

# AMELIA FANG
adventure

Coming soon!